EAT WHEN
YOU FEEL SAD

Zachary German

EAT WHEN
YOU FEEL SAD

Zachary German

Melville House Publishing
Brooklyn, New York

EAT WHEN YOU FEEL SAD

Melville House Publishing
145 Plymouth Street
Brooklyn, NY 11201

www.mhpbooks.com

ISBN: 978-1-933633-85-5

First Melville House Printing: December 2009

Book design by Kelly Blair

Printed in the United States of America

Library of Congress Cataloging-in-Publication Data

German, Zachary.
  Eat when you feel sad : a novel / Zachary German.
    p. cm.
  ISBN 978-1-933633-85-5
  I. Title.
  PS3607.E767E28 2010
  813'.6--dc22
                          2009045534

Robert is in his parents' house. He is in the living room. There are yarn cobwebs hanging from the ceiling. There are plastic spiders in the yarn cobwebs. Robert's parents wear costumes. Robert's parents' friends wear costumes. Robert wears a costume. He sits on a couch. He eats peanuts. He drinks soda. Robert eats small hotdogs.

Years later, Robert and Mark are in a video arcade. Mark plays *Silent Scope*. Robert looks at Mark. Robert says "Do you want to go?"

Mark says "Yeah. I'm going to die."

Robert says "Okay." In *Silent Scope*, Mark's character dies. Robert and Mark walk out of the video arcade. They walk into a record store. Robert looks at CDs by Sublime, Green Day, 311, Less Than Jake and Weezer. Robert looks at the CD *Neon Ballroom* by Silverchair. He thinks "I don't know if I should buy this." Robert walks to Mark. Robert says "Do you want to go?" Mark buys the album *Pinkerton* by Weezer. Robert and Mark walk out of the record store.

Robert walks into a classroom. He sits at a desk. Robert reads *Deadeye Dick* by Kurt Vonnegut. Casey walks to Robert. He stands in front of Robert. Casey says "So Robby, I heard you started, you know." Robert looks at Casey.

Robert says "Yeah?"

Casey says "Yeah man." He says "That's great man." Casey says "And about time, you know?"

Robert says "Yeah, I guess."

Casey says "I can see why you wouldn't want to talk about this. Just one word of advice man: baby oil."

Robert says "Thank you." Casey leaves. Robert looks at *Deadeye Dick*. He thinks "I wish Casey hadn't said that."

Robert and Mark are standing outside a movie theater. They are standing in a line. Robert and Mark are talking about girls in their school. Mark says "Erin has a really nice ass." Robert laughs quietly.

Robert says "You could put a cup on her ass." Mark laughs.

Mark says "What?"

Robert says "*You could put a cup on her ass.*" He says "I don't know, I think rappers say that or something. Like a big ass." Robert thinks "I'm surprised I can talk like this." Robert and Mark talk more. They are in the front of the line. There is a window. There is a man behind the window. The man is Indian. Mark says "One for *Fear.com*."

The man says "ID please."

Mark says "Um... I don't have it with me."

The man says "You have to be seventeen or accompanied by a parent or guardian to see R-rated movies."

Mark says "Oh yeah." Robert and Mark walk. It's bright. Mark says "That's some bullshit."

Robert says "Yeah."

Mark says "We should have asked to see that guy's green card." Robert laughs. Mark laughs.

The album *Enema of the State* by Blink 182 is playing. Robert is sitting on a couch. Lydia is sitting on the couch. Robert's heart is beating. Robert and Lydia talk. Robert thinks "It's easy to talk to Lydia." He looks at Lydia. Lydia leaves. Robert is sitting on the couch. The movie *Austin Powers in Goldmember* is playing on mute. Robert looks at *Austin Powers in Goldmember*. He looks at Mark. Mark is smoking pot. Robert thinks "Should I smoke pot?"

It's Christmas. Robert is in his parents' house. He is in the living room. Robert is sitting on a couch. His parents are there. His grandparents are there. His aunt and uncle are there. His other uncle is there. Robert picks up a wrapped package. He opens the package. The package contains the album *Oh, Inverted World* by The Shins on vinyl. Robert says "Thank you." He looks at his aunt and uncle. Robert's aunt smiles. Robert picks up a wrapped package. He opens the package. The package contains a Sub Pop label sampler CD.

Robert's aunt says "It came with the record." Robert nods.

Robert says "Thanks a lot." Everyone talks. Robert's grandparents leave. Robert's aunt and uncle leave. Robert's other uncle leaves. Robert's parents walk into their bedroom. Robert puts water into a tea kettle. He turns the stove on. Robert turns the stove off. He puts a tea bag into a mug. He pours water into the mug. Robert picks up the mug. He walks to his bedroom. He puts the Sub Pop label sampler CD into his computer. He listens to the Sub Pop label sampler CD. He thinks "I like the song 'Things I Don't Remember' by Ugly Casanova, 'Out of the Races and Onto the Tracks' by The Rapture, 'Bandages' by Hot Hot Heat, and 'Finish Line' by Rosie Thomas." Robert makes a playlist of those four songs. He lies on his bed. He sits up in his bed. He drinks tea. Robert listens to the playlist. He looks out the window. Snow is falling. It's warm.

Robert and Mark walk outside. There is snow. Robert and Mark smoke pot. They walk inside. Robert puts popcorn in the microwave. Mark sits on the couch. Robert sits on the couch. Robert and Mark watch *I Love the 80s*. They are near the fireplace. Robert puts his hand next to his face. He turns his face away from Mark. Robert thinks "Before I felt okay but now I feel like I can't. Something. I don't know. I'm going to act normal." Robert looks at the TV. Mark looks at the TV. The microwave beeps. A commercial comes on. Robert stands up. He looks at the TV. He thinks "I like this commercial." Robert sits on the couch. A commercial comes on. Robert stands up. He walks to the kitchen. He takes the popcorn out of the microwave. He puts the popcorn in a large bowl. He says "Do you want anything to drink?"

Mark says "OJ please." Robert thinks "I don't have school tomorrow." Robert pours orange juice into two glasses. He walks to the living room. He puts two glasses of orange juice and a large bowl of popcorn on the coffee table. Robert sits on the couch. Mark says "Thanks." *I Love the 80s* is on TV. Someone on *I Love the 80s* says something about Morrissey.

Robert is in a community center. There is music. People are standing. People are dancing. People are sitting in chairs. Robert is sitting in a chair. He's standing. He's talking to people. Robert is in the bathroom. He pees. Robert washes his hands. He is in the community center. The song "E.I." by Nelly is playing. Robert is outside. He is standing with Mark. Mark's dad's car comes. Robert and Mark get into Mark's dad's car. They are in front of Robert's parents' house. Robert says "Thank you." He gets out of the car. He is standing in front of his parents' house. Robert's parents' dog barks. Robert walks inside. He turns the stove on. He walks to his parents' bedroom. He stands in the doorway. Robert says "Hello." He talks to his parents. Robert thinks "I want my parents to die, kind of." Robert walks to his bedroom. He looks at the book *Tender is the Night* by F. Scott Fitzgerald. Robert walks down stairs. He turns the stove off. He puts a tea bag into a mug. He pours water into the mug. Robert picks up the mug. He walks to the computer room. He signs onto AOL Instant Messenger. Lydia instant messages Robert.

Lydia says "Hi."

Robert says "Hi." He thinks "I want to watch TV." Robert says "I have to go." He signs off of AOL Instant Messenger. He walks to the living room. Robert sits on the couch. He drinks tea. He turns on the TV. *King of the Hill* is on TV. Robert looks at the TV. Robert is asleep. He is awake. He walks to his bedroom. He thinks "My life is getting better." He is asleep.

Robert and Mark walk into a store. Mark buys a wooden box. Robert looks at the box. He looks at the cash register. Robert frowns. He thinks "Is Mark stupid?" He thinks "Am I stupid?" Robert and Mark walk out of the store. They walk into a bookstore. They look at magazines. Robert looks at the counter. There is a young man behind the counter. Robert walks to the counter. He says "Do you have anything by Charles Bukowski?"

The young man says "Yes." He walks from behind the counter to the front of the counter. He says "Right this way." The young man walks to the back of the store. Robert and Mark walk to the back of the store. The young man turns around. The young man says "Bukowski, he's great, man."

Robert says "Yeah. Yeah I've only read a little, but yeah."

Mark says "I've only read a little too. But yeah."

The young man says "Um." The young man points at one of the shelves. He says "Here's his fiction." The young man points at one of the shelves. He says "Here's his poetry." Robert looks at the young man's shirt. Robert sees a laminated badge that says *Dave*.

Robert says "Is your name Dave?"

Dave says "Yeah."

Robert says "I'm Robert."

Mark says "I'm Mark." Dave asks Robert and Mark if they go to the high school that they go to.

Robert says "Yeah, we're sophomores." Mark looks at Robert. Robert thinks "I'm a freshman." He thinks "It just seemed easier to say that we're both sophomores." Robert says "How about you?"

Dave says "I graduated a few years ago but yeah I went to school here. It sucked."

Robert and Mark say "Yeah."

Dave says "If you guys want to just take shit from here you can. Just so you know. Like I do it all the time."

Mark says "Good to know." He smiles. Robert smiles.

Robert says "Thanks a lot, man."

Dave says "Yeah no problem. Just be careful if you see anyone old at the counter. Anyone under twenty-five or so, thirty or so shouldn't give you a problem. See you later." Dave leaves.

Robert says "He seems cool." Robert unzips his book bag.

Mark says "His badge was a Dave Matthews Band button with the last two words taped over."

Robert says "Oh yeah." Robert puts the book *South of No North* by Charles Bukowski into his book bag. Robert puts the book *The Days Run Away Like Wild Horses Over The Hills* by Charles Bukowski into his book bag. He picks up the book *The Immoralist* by André Gide. Robert thinks "Best title ever." Robert holds *The Immoralist* towards Mark. Mark looks at *The Immoralist*. Robert says "Best title ever." He puts *The Immoralist* into his book bag. Mark puts books into his bag. Robert zips his book bag. Robert and Mark each pick up a copy of Dennis Cooper's *Period*. They walk to the front of the store. Robert and Mark each buy a copy of Dennis Cooper's *Period*. Robert and Mark walk outside. Mark calls his dad. Robert and Mark are standing outside. It's warm. Mark's dad's car comes. Robert and Mark get into Mark's dad's car. Mark tells his dad about the things that he bought. Mark's dad smokes cigarettes. Mark's dad smells like red wine. They are in front of Mark's parents' house. They get out of the car. Mark's dad pees on the lawn. Robert and Mark walk into Mark's parents' house. Robert and Mark walk up stairs. They walk into Mark's bedroom. Robert lies on the floor. Mark signs on to AOL Instant Messenger.

Mark says "Why did you tell that guy that you were a sophomore?"

Robert says "I don't know."

Robert is dreaming. In his dream, Robert and his English teacher are standing between a chalkboard and a white screen, in the front of Robert's English class. Robert touches his English teacher's breasts over her blouse. He thinks "She probably got her blouse at Fashion Bug." Robert kisses his English teacher's face. He says "You're hot." Robert winces. He touches his English teacher's crotch over her khaki pants. Robert pushes his middle finger and his forefinger up. Robert's English teacher's head tilts back. Robert kisses his English teacher's neck. Robert's English teacher makes a sound.

Robert and Mark are playing *South Park: Chef's Love Shack* on Sega Dreamcast. Mark says "This is funny." Robert picks up a glass. He drinks orange juice. His hand is cold. Robert and Mark walk to the computer room. They sit down. Robert signs onto AOL Instant Messenger. He signs off of AOL Instant Messenger. Robert and Mark walk to the living room. Robert turns on the TV. Mark says "Give me the remote." Robert hands Mark the remote. Mark changes the channel. Cinemax is on TV. *As Good As It Gets* is on Cinemax. Mark says "Nevermind." He says "Sometimes there's porn on here." Mark hands Robert the remote. Robert changes the channel. *MTV Jams* is on TV. The music video "Big Pimpin'" by Jay-Z featuring UGK is on TV. Mark walks to the computer room. Robert walks to the bathroom.

He washes his hands. He brushes his teeth. He puts water in his hair. He rubs a towel against his hair.

Robert is playing *Civilization II* on his computer. The album *Moondance* by Van Morrison is playing. Lydia instant messages Robert. Lydia says "Hey."

Robert says "Hey." Robert plays *Civilization II*.

Lydia says "What are you doing?"

Robert says "Nothing." He thinks "Should I say 'You'?"

Robert looks at Lydia's MySpace page. He sets an away message on AOL Instant Messenger. He walks to the living room. Robert turns on the TV.

There is a package on Robert's parents' front porch. Robert picks up the package. He looks at it. Robert walks into his parents' house. He walks into his bedroom. He opens the package. Robert holds the book *Life Against Death: The Psychoanalytic Meaning of History* by Norman O. Brown. He looks at the cover. He touches the cover. Robert thinks "The cover looks good." Robert looks out the window. He walks to the living room. He turns on the TV. He walks to the kitchen. He opens the freezer. He looks at the freezer. Robert picks up a package of veggie burger patties. He takes a veggie burger patty from the package. Robert puts the package into the freezer. He closes the freezer. Robert puts the veggie burger patty into the microwave. He presses buttons on the microwave. The microwave is illuminated. Robert looks at his parents' dog. His parents' dog is moving quickly. Robert thinks "I can't see the dog clearly. It's moving too quickly." Robert opens the back door. He walks onto the deck. Robert's parents' dog walks onto the deck. Robert's parents' dog walks onto the grass. Robert's parents' dog runs. Robert looks at his parents' dog. Robert walks inside. He looks at the microwave. He looks at the TV.

Robert is in a classroom. He is sitting at a desk. He thinks "I should ask to use the bathroom and then walk outside." He thinks "What's outside?" Robert thinks "Nevermind." Robert thinks "I should just not come to this class tomorrow. I should go to English and then after English I should walk outside. It doesn't matter. There's nothing outside probably." Robert looks at his biology teacher. Robert's biology teacher is obese. Robert's biology teacher passes out a paper. The words "TEST TUES. STUDY!!" are written on the top of the first page of the paper. Biology information is printed on both sides of the paper. Robert puts his head on his desk. He lifts his head up. Robert looks at the door.

Robert is in his car. He is in a parking lot. The album *The Earth Is Not A Cold Dead Place* by Explosions In The Sky is playing. He looks at a woman. The woman is pushing a baby carriage. A boy is standing near the woman. The boy is holding a cell phone. Robert looks at the boy. Robert looks at his own cell phone. Robert looks at the CD case for *The Earth Is Not A Cold Dead Place*. Robert thinks "I want to be drunk." He thinks "I want to masturbate onto a person." Robert turns off his car. He gets out of his car. He walks to the back of his car. He walks to the driver side door. He opens his car's door. He turns his car on. He closes the windows. Robert turns his car off. Robert closes his car's door. He locks his car. He walks to the edge of the parking lot. He looks at the highway.

A year later, Robert is lying down. He isn't wearing a shirt. Alison is lying down. Alison isn't wearing a shirt. Robert is touching Alison's breasts. Robert and Alison are kissing. Robert thinks "I should break up with Alison." He thinks "No." Robert and Alison stop kissing. Robert kisses Alison's breasts. Alison makes a sound. She puts her hand on Robert's crotch. Robert is wearing jeans. Alison unbuttons Robert's jeans. She puts her hand under Robert's underpants. Alison touches Robert's penis. Robert thinks "I should break up with Alison." He thinks "No." He thinks "I don't know." He thinks "I'd probably regret it. Something. I should wait." Robert kisses Alison's mouth. He unbuttons Alison's jeans. He puts his hand under Alison's underpants. Alison makes a sound.

Robert is driving. The album *Sing Along with Acid House Kings* by Acid House Kings is playing. There is a deli. Robert turns towards the deli's parking lot. Robert parks his car. He looks at the other cars in the parking lot. Robert thinks "I hope I don't see anyone I know." He walks into the deli. Robert orders a vegetable hoagie. He pays for the vegetable hoagie. Robert looks at the vegetable hoagie. He thinks "I'm stupid." Robert says "I don't need a bag." Robert picks up the vegetable hoagie. He walks to his car.

Robert and Alison have sex. They finish having sex. Alison opens and closes her eyes. A sound comes from Alison's nose. A sound comes from Alison's mouth. Robert says "Are you crying?"

Alison says "Yes." She touches her nose.

Robert says "Why?"

Alison says "Um." Robert thinks "Should I touch Alison's arm or something?"

Robert says "What is it?"

Alison says "Um." Robert stretches his legs.

Robert says "Are you still crying?"

Alison says "Yes."

Robert says "Why?"

Alison says "Well." Alison says "I used to... I used to think I was a lesbian because I didn't want for sex to hurt."

Robert says "Oh." Robert looks at Alison. Alison looks at Robert. She stands up. She puts on a nightgown. Alison walks to the door. Robert says "Alison." Alison leaves. Robert looks at the ceiling. He stands up. He puts on underwear. He puts on jeans. He puts on a t-shirt. Robert lies on Alison's bed. He stands up.

Robert is driving. The album *Ready to Die* by The Notorious B.I.G. is playing. Robert thinks "*Ready to Die* is better than *Life After Death*. Biggie would have gotten worse as time went by. I'm still sad that he died kind of. No, I'm not." Robert pulls his car over to the side of the road. He turns off his car. He gets out of his car. He locks his car. He walks into the woods. Robert pees. He looks at a tree. Robert touches the tree. Robert says "Fuck." He thinks "I have memories of throwing rocks at dumpsters." Robert picks up a leaf. He thinks "I'm going to feel bad forever I guess." It's raining. Robert runs. He kicks his car's front passenger side tire. He gets into his car. He sits in his car.

Robert is in his parents' house. He is in the kitchen. He looks at the microwave. The microwave is illuminated. There is a veggie burger patty in the microwave. Robert looks at a plate. There is a bun on the plate. He opens the refrigerator. Robert picks up ketchup. He looks at a bag of lettuce. He picks up the bag of lettuce. Robert closes the refrigerator. He puts lettuce on the bun. The microwave makes a sound. Robert opens the microwave. He takes the veggie burger patty out of the microwave. He closes the microwave. He puts the veggie burger patty on the lettuce. He puts ketchup on the veggie burger patty. Robert opens the refrigerator. He puts the bag of lettuce in the refrigerator. He puts the ketchup in the refrigerator.

Robert is in his car. He is driving. There are three black trash bags in Robert's car. There are clothes in the black trash bags. There are six cardboard boxes in Robert's car. There are books in the cardboard boxes. There are other things in Robert's car. Robert turns on the radio. He turns off the radio. He looks at the rear view mirror. He looks at the black trash bags. He looks at the cardboard boxes. He looks at other things. There is a tollbooth. Robert lowers his window. He hands two one-dollar bills to a man. The man says "Thank you."

Robert says "Thank you." Robert is on a bridge. He turns on the radio. He turns off the radio. Robert is in a city. Robert is driving slowly. He parks his car. Robert gets out of his car. He takes his cell phone out of his pocket. He calls Jim. Robert says "Hey man, I'm outside." Robert looks at the sky. The sky is gray. Robert thinks "I feel pretty good about this." A door opens. Jim is outside. Robert says "Hey Jim."

Jim says "Hey Robert." He walks to Robert. He says "You want some help moving your stuff in?"

Robert says "That'd be great."

Robert is lying on Alison's bed. The album *Something About Airplanes* by Death Cab for Cutie is playing. Alison walks into her bedroom. She's wearing a towel. Her hair is wet. Alison sits on her bed. Robert touches Alison's leg. Robert smiles. Alison smiles.

Six months later, Robert is riding his bike. Robert locks his bike to a parking meter. Robert walks into a Chinese restaurant. He says "Table for one please." A Chinese woman shows Robert to a table. Robert sits on a chair. A Chinese woman hands Robert a menu. Robert orders food.

He drinks tea. He walks to the bathroom. Robert pees. He walks to his table. Robert pays for the food. Robert walks outside. He thinks "I shouldn't eat Chinese food." He thinks "I feel good while I'm eating Chinese food, but I feel bad later." He thinks "Winter is coming." Robert rides his bike. He stops riding his bike. Robert locks his bike to a street sign. He walks into a library. He looks at shelves. Robert picks up the book *Heavy Water and Other Stories* by Martin Amis. Robert sits on a chair. He reads two stories. He thinks "Martin Amis." He thinks "What the fuck?" Robert closes *Heavy Water and Other Stories*. He looks at the cover. He puts *Heavy Water and Other Stories* on a shelf. Robert walks outside. He thinks "Winter." Robert rides his bike. He is in front of his building. Robert walks into his building. He walks up stairs. He walks into his apartment. Robert takes a shower. He is lying on his bed. Robert thinks "Okay."

The song "A Minor Place" by "Bonnie 'Prince' Billy" is playing. Robert's cell phone rings. Robert looks at his cell phone. He picks up his cell phone. Robert says "Hello."

Tom says "We're down stairs."

Robert says "Okay, I'll be right down." Robert stands up. He walks out of his bedroom. He walks out of his apartment. Robert walks down stairs. He opens his building's door. He says "Hiya."

Tom says "Hey." He says the word slowly.

Nancy says "Hi."

Paul says "Hi."

Robert says "Hi." Robert, Tom, Paul and Nancy walk up stairs. They walk into Robert's apartment. They walk into Robert's bedroom.

Tom says "We saw *Snakes on a Plane.*" Nancy looks at Robert's laptop computer. The song "Heartbeats" by The Knife is playing.

Robert says "How was it?"

Tom says "You should play the live version of this, it's so much better." Nancy looks at Robert's laptop computer.

Nancy says "He doesn't have it."

Tom says "You suck dude."

Robert says "Yeah I know."

Paul says "It wasn't very good." Paul looks at his shoes. Robert looks at Paul's shoes.

Tom says "Yeah it wasn't really anything. I thought it would be a lot funnier."

Robert says "Huh."

Tom says "It was funny for like the first twenty-five minutes. Some guy got his dick bitten off, or something."

Robert says "That's cool." Robert lies on his bed. He sits up in his bed. "Shoulder Lean" by Young Dro featuring T.I. is playing. Robert says *"Make your shoulder lean."* He says "What's everybody doing tonight?" Robert looks at the ceiling. He thinks "The ceiling is really dirty."

Paul says "There's a party." Paul tells Robert where the party is. Paul says the party is for his friend's friend who just got into medical school.

Robert says "Yeah I'll go. Yeah alright." Tom says that he's too tired to go to the party. He says that he has work tomorrow.

Tom says "Jim's gonna get home from work in a little bit, is it alright if I just hang out here until he gets back?"

Robert says "Yeah of course." Tom, Paul and Nancy leave Robert's bedroom. Robert changes his clothes. It's summer. Robert walks outside. Paul and Nancy are smoking cigarettes on the stoop. They finish smoking cigarettes. Robert, Paul and Nancy say goodbye to Tom. They walk to Nancy's car. They sit in Nancy's car. Nancy drives. A commercial hip-hop radio station is playing. Nancy parks her car. Robert, Paul and Nancy get out of Nancy's car. They walk into a beer store. Robert buys a six-pack of sixteen-ounce cans of Pabst Blue Ribbon beer. Paul buys a forty-ounce bottle of Milwaukee's Best beer. Nancy buys a forty-ounce bottle of Milwaukee's Best beer. They walk outside. They walk to Nancy's car. They sit in her car. Nancy drives. Nancy parks her car. They get out of Nancy's car. They walk to the party. The song "Crimewave" by Crystal Castles and Health is playing. People are dancing. There are jello shots. Robert says "This party is funny."

Paul says "Yeah." Robert drinks two sixteen-ounce cans of Pabst Blue Ribbon beer. Paul drinks most of his forty-ounce bottle of Milwaukee's Best beer. Nancy drinks most of her forty-ounce bottle of Milwaukee's Best beer. Paul talks to his friend whose friend's party it is. Robert, Paul and Nancy walk outside. They ask someone directions to the nearest Chinese restaurant. They walk to the Chinese restaurant. They walk into the Chinese restaurant. Robert buys a Phillies Blunt and a homemade iced tea. He orders a vegetable lo mein. Paul orders a vegetable lo mein. Nancy buys a homemade lemonade. Robert, Paul and Nancy walk outside. They sit on steps. Robert smokes a Phillies blunt. Paul and Nancy smoke cigarettes. Robert thinks "Smoking." He laughs. Paul says "What?" Robert doesn't say anything. Robert and Paul walk into the Chinese restaurant. They pick up their food. Robert and Paul walk outside. They sit on steps. Robert and Paul eat vegetable lo mein. Nancy smokes a cigarette. Robert looks at his sixteen-ounce cans of Pabst Blue Ribbon beer. Robert, Paul and Nancy walk to Nancy's car. They drive to Robert's building. They walk into Robert's building. They walk up stairs. They walk into Robert's apartment. Jim and Tom are watching the David Bowie video collection. Robert, Paul and Nancy tell Jim and Tom about the party.

Robert says "These songs are too late or something. I don't know. These songs suck."

Tom says "Yeah." He looks at the TV. He says "Do you want to watch something else?"

Robert says "I don't care." Jim says that they should watch *Little Otek*. Jim and Tom look for *Little Otek*. Tom finds *Little Otek*. Tom puts *Little Otek* into the VCR. Everyone looks at the TV. Robert thinks "It's hard to read the subtitles. I'm drunk, I guess." Robert is sitting near Paul. Robert is drinking from a sixteen-ounce can of Pabst Blue Ribbon beer. Robert asks Paul if he wants one.

Paul says "Yeah I think I would like that." Robert hands Paul a sixteen-ounce can of Pabst Blue Ribbon beer. Paul says "Thank you." Robert looks at the ceiling. Robert thinks "Okay." He thinks "Okay." He thinks "Okay." He thinks "I've been thinking this for a while." He thinks "Okay." Robert picks up a piece of paper. He picks up a pen. He writes "I LIKE YOU AND WANT TO BE BOYFRIENDS" on the piece of paper. He hands the piece of paper to Paul. Paul looks at Robert. Paul says "Yeah." He says "I feel that way too." Paul is smiling. Robert isn't smiling. Robert looks at the ceiling. Robert looks at Paul. Robert smiles. Robert looks at the ceiling. He looks at the TV.

Robert says "Do you want to go to my room?" Paul nods. Robert stands up. Paul stands up. Robert picks up two sixteen-ounce cans of Pabst Blue Ribbon beer. Robert looks at the people in the living room. Robert and Paul walk into Robert's bedroom. Robert puts the two sixteen-ounce cans of Pabst Blue Ribbon beer on the floor. He looks at them. Robert and Paul lie on Robert's bed. Robert says "Do you want to split a beer?" Paul nods. Robert picks up a sixteen-ounce can of Pabst Blue Ribbon beer. He opens it. He sits up in his bed. Paul sits up in Robert's bed. Paul and Robert drink beer. They talk. Paul talks about a woman he works with.

Paul says "She's just, like, so ghetto. Like when that song "Chicken Noodle Soup" comes on the radio she, like, sings along. I don't know. She's... really honest." Paul says something about college. He says something about his family, how they don't celebrate birthdays. Robert thinks "Maybe he doesn't know what I meant earlier." He thinks "No, nevermind." Paul stops talking. No one's talking. It's quiet. Robert finishes drinking the sixteen-ounce can of Pabst Blue Ribbon beer. He puts it on the floor.

Robert says "I've never done anything like this before."

Paul says "Like what?" Tears form in Robert's eyes. He thinks "Okay."

Robert says "Like with a boy. It's just a lot different."

Paul says "We're not really doing anything."

Robert says "Can I kiss you?"

Paul says "Okay." Robert kisses Paul on the lips. He feels Paul's facial hair against his lips. He thinks "I'm not gay." Robert and Paul talk. Robert picks up a sixteen-ounce can of Pabst Blue Ribbon beer. He opens it.

Paul says "I think I'm going to go."

Robert says "I'm sorry." Paul stands up. Robert stands up. Paul puts on his shoes. Robert says "You're okay walking home?"

Paul says "Yeah, it's not far." Robert opens his bedroom door. No one is in the living room.

Robert says "Do you want me to walk you home?"

Paul says "No, Robert."

Robert says "Okay." They walk into the living room. Robert says "Do you want anything? A glass of water?"

Paul says "No." Robert looks at Paul. Robert frowns. Paul opens the apartment door. He walks out of Robert's apartment. Robert walks out of his apartment. Robert and Paul walk down stairs. They walk outside. It's warm. Robert thinks "I'm alive." He thinks "I can do whatever I want pretty much."

Paul says "I'm going home now."

Robert says "I'm so sorry."

Paul says "It's okay." Paul leaves. Robert walks inside. He closes the door. He walks up stairs. He walks into his apartment. He walks into his bedroom. Robert watches the live version of "Heartbeats" by The Knife on YouTube. Robert lies on his bed. He calls Alison. He stands up. He leans against a wall. Robert thinks "I wish I had cigarettes sort of." He plays the song "Stockholm Syndrome" by Yo La Tengo. He lies on his bed.

Robert is in a large loft apartment. There is a high ceiling. There is a stage. There is a bar. Robert is wearing white Puma sneakers. He is wearing black jeans from American Apparel. He is wearing a pink t-shirt with a drawing of a rabbit and the words "The Ballet." He is wearing contact lenses. Robert buys a can of Pabst Blue Ribbon beer. He drinks it. Robert touches his hair. Robert is sitting on a couch. He stands up. He looks at a young woman. Robert buys a can of Pabst Blue Ribbon beer. He stands in a line. A band comes on stage. Some of the people in front of Robert leave the line. A young man walks out of the bathroom.

Robert walks into the bathroom. He looks at himself in the mirror. He looks at his eyes in the mirror. Robert washes his face. Robert hears a knock on the bathroom door. Robert says "Just a minute." He rubs a paper towel against his face. He thinks "God." He walks out of the bathroom. Robert sits on the couch. There is a band onstage. Robert is the only person on the couch. Robert walks outside. People are smoking cigarettes. It's cold. Robert smokes a cigarette. He walks inside. Robert buys a can of Pabst Blue Ribbon beer. He sits on the couch. There is a couple making out on the other end of the couch. Robert looks at his shoes. He looks at his cell phone. Robert drinks Pabst Blue Ribbon beer. The Black Lips come on stage. Robert stands up. He stands near the stage. The Black Lips play. Robert thinks "The Black Lips have gotten consistently shittier their entire career. Their discography is an apt metaphor for my life." Robert smiles. The Black Lips stop playing. Robert walks outside. He stands near a corner. He gets on a bus. Robert looks at a newspaper. He gets off the bus. He walks into his building. He walks up stairs. He walks into his apartment. Robert walks into his bedroom. He turns on the TV. He looks at the TV.

It's Thanksgiving. Robert is walking. He walks past H&M. He walks past United Colors of Benetton. He walks past Kenneth Cole New York. Robert is in front of a Chinese restaurant. He reads the menu. He walks into the Chinese restaurant. There is an old Chinese woman. Robert looks at the Chinese woman. He says "One, please." There are men wearing business suits. The old Chinese woman nods.

The old Chinese woman says "Of course." She walks to a table. Robert walks to the table. The old Chinese woman puts a menu on the table. She walks away. Robert puts his book bag under the table. He sits on a chair. A young Chinese woman pours tea into a cup. She places fried noodles, duck sauce and spicy mustard on Robert's table. The young Chinese woman walks away. It's warm. Robert thinks "It's nice here." He eats fried noodles. The young Chinese woman walks to Robert's table. Robert orders Chinese food. The young Chinese woman walks away. Robert drinks tea. He eats fried noodles. He dips a fried noodle into duck sauce. He dips the same fried noodle into spicy mustard. He looks at the spicy mustard. He eats the fried noodle. The young Chinese woman brings Robert Chinese food. Robert eats Chinese food. Robert walks to the bathroom. He looks at himself in the mirror. He has acne on his face. Robert puts water on his face. He touches his face. Robert puts more water on his face. He rubs a paper towel against his face. He walks out of the bathroom. He walks to his table. He sits on the chair.

The young Chinese woman says "All done?"

Robert says "Yes. Thank you."

The young Chinese woman says "It was good?"

Robert says "Yes. Very good. Thank you." The young Chinese woman places the bill on Robert's table.

The young Chinese woman says "Thank you."

Robert is looking at pictures of shower filters on the internet. He looks at descriptions of shower filters. He stands up. He bends over. He touches his calves. He sits down. He looks at pictures of shower filters. He stands up. Robert walks out of his bedroom. He walks into the kitchen. He opens the refrigerator. He picks up broccoli. Robert closes the refrigerator. He sits on a chair. He puts broccoli on the kitchen table. He looks at broccoli. Robert thinks "I should get a better job so I can live alone." He stands up. Robert thinks "I guess I could live alone now if I really wanted." It's cold. Robert picks up broccoli. He opens the refrigerator. He puts broccoli in the refrigerator. He closes the refrigerator. Robert walks to his bedroom.

Robert is in his parents' house. The album *The Adventures of Ghosthorse and Stillborn* by CocoRosie is playing. Robert checks his email. He has one new email. Robert thinks "It was fun being younger because it didn't matter what I did, or it didn't matter right away anyway. I think it didn't matter. Either way." Robert reads a review of *The Adventures of Ghosthorse and Stillborn* on Pitchfork. He reads a review of *The Adventures of Ghosthorse and Stillborn* on The Fanzine. Robert stands up. It's dark. It's three a.m. Robert walks to the living room. He eats hummus and corn chips. He watches three episodes of *The Office*.

Robert is awake. He stands up. He disconnects his cell phone from his cell phone charger. He looks at his cell phone. He looks at his laptop computer. Robert turns on his laptop computer. He listens to the song "Rawtoon" by Lil Wayne. He takes off his clothes. He takes the sheets off his bed. He lies on his bed. He looks out the window. He takes a shower. He checks his email. He has one new email. The email is from Paul. Robert opens the email. The email says "how've you been? things are okay here, break is this next week and wondering if you wanted to do something. animal collective is playing wednesday, i'm not sure if it's sold out. hope you're well."

Robert's cell phone vibrates. Robert looks at his cell phone. Robert says "Hello?"

Steve says "Hey." Robert and Steve talk. Steve says "Do you want to come over?"

Robert says "Sure, yeah."

Steve says "Cool." Robert walks to Steve's building. Steve is sitting on the steps outside. Ted is sitting with Steve. Steve and Ted are drinking beer. Robert sits with Steve and Ted. Robert drinks beer. Kelly and Abby come. Robert thinks "They're drunk already." Robert, Steve, Ted, Kelly and Abby walk into Steve's building. They walk up stairs. They walk into Steve's apartment. Robert drinks beer. Steve and Ted drink beer. Kelly and Abby drink vodka mixed with iced tea from a water bottle. Robert drinks vodka mixed with iced tea from a water bottle. Ted leaves. Robert, Steve, Kelly and Abby walk outside. They sit on the steps outside. Steve and Abby walk inside. Robert and Kelly are alone.

Robert says "Can I put my arm around you?"

Kelly says "Yeah."

Robert is in American Apparel. He thinks "If I worked here my life would be different, or I would need to have a different life in order to work here, or something." He picks up a pink v-neck t-shirt. He holds it to his chest. He thinks "I'm really not confident with how I look, or how I would look wearing this pink v-neck t-shirt. Wow." Robert puts on a gray and blue pullover sweatshirt with the colors divided diagonally. He takes off the sweatshirt. Robert thinks "I wish I was in my bedroom." The song "Out of the Races and Onto the Tracks" by The Rapture is playing. Robert thinks "2003." He closes his eyes for a few seconds. He rubs his sleeve against his face. He walks to where there is underwear. He picks up a pair of underwear. He looks at the underwear. He picks up four pairs of underwear. He looks at them. He is holding five pairs of underwear. He stands in a line.

Robert checks his email. He has a Facebook message from Kelly. It says "robert, i left my phone at my parents' house. i figured you have been trying to call me since we were supposed to do something today. i cant cause i have a 5 page paper due tomorrow. are you free next weekend anytime? or thursday (i dont have classes)." Robert thinks "I'm not sure if she likes me. I thought she liked me before." Robert plays the song "Don't Die In Me" by Mirah. He thinks "I'm wearing stupid clothes." Robert plays the song "Sara Smile" by Hall and Oates. He looks at a pornographic video. He mutes the sound on the pornographic video. He listens to Hall and Oates. Robert takes off his clothes. He jerks his penis. In the video, a young woman takes off her pants. Robert jerks his penis. In the video, a man's hand touches the young woman's vagina. The man's hand is hairy. Robert looks at his own hand. Robert's hand is not hairy. Robert checks his email. He jerks his penis. He has no new email. In the video, something happens. Robert ejaculates. He stands up.

Robert walks into a store. He looks at cigarettes. He buys a pack of Dunhill cigarettes. Robert walks outside. He walks to a concert. He walks inside. A band is playing. The band stops playing. Robert walks outside. He sits on a low stone wall. He smokes a cigarette. The guitar player from the band walks outside. He says "Do you have a light?"

Robert says "Sure yeah." Robert takes a pack of matches out of his pocket. He hands the pack of matches to the guitar player. Robert says "That was good. I like your thing."

The guitar player says "Thanks." He hands Robert the matches. Robert and the guitar player talk. Someone says that Chris Garneau is about to play. Robert and the guitar player walk inside. Chris Garneau plays. Chris Garneau stops playing. Robert walks outside. Robert walks to his building. He walks into his building. He walks up stairs. He walks into his apartment. Robert thinks "I want to smoke another cigarette." He drinks a glass of water. He walks to his bedroom. He checks his email. He has four new emails. Robert reads his new emails. He writes two emails.

Robert's knees are on either side of Kelly's midsection. His penis is near Kelly's head. Kelly's hand is touching Robert's penis. Robert's penis is semi-erect. Robert is naked. Kelly is naked. Robert is wearing socks. Kelly is wearing one sock. Robert is asleep. He is awake. Robert looks at Kelly. He says "Kelly." Robert lies on Kelly's bed. He says "Hi."
Kelly says "Hi." Robert kisses Kelly.

Robert is standing in his bedroom. It is night. Robert looks at his bed. Robert lies on his bed. He looks at the ceiling. He looks at his curtains. The wind blows his curtains gently. Robert plays the song "Chickfactor" by Belle & Sebastian. He turns off his bedside lamp. He thinks "My job is okay." He is asleep.

Robert rides his bike to Kelly's building. Steve and Abby are outside. They are smoking cigarettes. Robert says "Hi."
Steve says "Hey Robert." Robert, Steve and Abby talk.
Abby says "She's in there."
Robert says "Thanks." He says "Have a good night." Robert walks inside. He walks up stairs. He walks into Kelly's apartment. He leans his bike against Kelly's bike. Robert walks down the hall. The bathroom light is on. Robert walks into Kelly's bedroom. He takes off his shirt. He takes off his jeans. He takes off his socks. Robert lies on Kelly's bed. He touches his face. His face touches his shoulder. Kelly walks into her bedroom. Robert sits up in Kelly's bed. Kelly closes the door. It's dark.
Kelly says "How did you get here so quick?"

Robert says "I rode my bike."

Kelly says "Oh." Kelly is wearing a towel. Kelly takes off the towel. Robert looks at the wall. Kelly puts on a nightgown. Robert looks at the wall. Kelly lies on her bed. Robert looks at Kelly. Kelly smells like whiskey. She smells like toothpaste. Kelly looks at Robert. Kelly says "Hi."

Robert says "Hi."

Kelly says "How are you?"

Robert says "Oh you know. I don't know." He says "How are you?" Kelly laughs. She looks at Robert. Kelly opens her mouth. She closes her mouth. Kelly kisses Robert on the nose. She laughs. Robert laughs. Robert kisses Kelly on the nose. He puts his hand on Kelly's side. Kelly moves closer to Robert. She makes a small sound. Kelly moves her face towards Robert's mouth. She kisses Robert's mouth. Robert kisses Kelly on the neck. Kelly makes a small sound. Robert moves his hand further down Kelly's body.

Robert is holding a black plastic bag. Robert walks into his bedroom. He looks at his cat. Robert closes his bedroom door. He touches his cat. Robert plays the album *They Might Be Giants* by They Might Be Giants. He turns down the volume. Robert takes a six-pack of eleven-point-six-ounce bottles of Elephant malt liquor out of the black plastic bag. He looks at the six-pack of eleven-point-six-ounce bottles of Elephant malt liquor. Robert touches one of the bottles. Robert's fingers become moist. Robert opens one of the bottles of Elephant malt liquor. He looks out the window. He sits on his bed. His legs are straight. His back is against the wall. Robert takes off his shirt. He throws the shirt onto the floor. It's eight p.m. Robert looks out the window. The sun is out. Robert looks at the park across the street. He looks at people in the park across the street. He thinks "I'm sorry that everyone has problems. I don't know what to do. I'm vegan." Robert drinks Elephant malt liquor. His eyes open and close. Robert plays the song "Anthems for a Seventeen Year-Old Girl" by Broken Social Scene. It's warm. Robert thinks "I feel okay." He drinks Elephant malt liquor. He thinks "I want to call someone." He rubs a pillowcase against his eyes. He drinks Elephant malt liquor. He thinks "I like Broken Social Scene." The song "Cause = Time" by Broken Social Scene is playing. Robert thinks "I'm glad I don't have any disabilities." Robert finishes drinking Elephant malt liquor. Robert is asleep.

Robert is lying on his bed. He is wearing white underwear. He is wearing blue socks. Robert's cat is touching Robert's leg. There are no sheets on Robert's bed. Robert is reading *My Loose Thread* by Dennis Cooper. He places *My Loose Thread* on his nightstand. Robert looks at his nightstand. He thinks "I like my nightstand."

Robert is in a library. Robert is reading *Voices from the Street* by Philip K. Dick. Robert thinks "I don't know if this book is good." He thinks "I don't know." Robert looks around the library. He thinks "Everyone in the library is black but me."

He places *Voices from the Street* on the table. Robert picks up his book bag. He takes the case for his laptop computer out of his book bag. He takes his laptop computer out of its case. He places his laptop computer on the table. Robert puts the case for his laptop computer into his book bag. Robert opens his laptop computer. He turns on his laptop computer. He connects to the internet. He checks his email. He has two new emails. He looks at three blogs. One of the blogs has a new post. Robert writes a comment on the post. The comment is "i think joy williams' novels are bad." Robert turns off his laptop computer. He puts his laptop computer into its case. He puts the case for his laptop computer into his book bag. Robert walks outside. He walks to 7-Eleven. He buys salsa. Robert walks to his building. He walks into his building. He walks up stairs. He walks into his apartment. Robert makes rice and beans. He puts salsa on the rice and beans. He eats it. He cries loudly. He looks at his cat. Robert says "Fuck, I suck." His speech is distorted by his crying. Robert laughs. He is still crying loudly. Robert lies on the couch. He thinks "My life is okay. My life is under control." Robert stands up. He washes dishes. Robert moves a fan from the kitchen to the living room. He points the fan towards the couch. He turns on the fan. He lies on the couch. He stands up. He walks to the bathroom. He takes a shower. He walks to his bedroom. He lies on his bed. There is a glass of water next to Robert's bed. Robert drinks from the glass of water. Robert is lying on his bed.

Robert is writing an email to Sam. He thinks "I like Sam a lot more than Sam likes me, probably."

Robert is lying on his bed. He calls his cousin. He doesn't leave a voicemail. He scrolls through his cell phone's phonebook. He thinks "Who are these people?" He thinks "No, I know who they are." Robert deletes some numbers from his cell phone's phonebook. He looks at his laptop computer. He looks at his cat.

Robert's cell phone rings. Robert looks at his cell phone. Robert picks up his cell phone. His cell phone says "lydia s." Robert answers his cell phone. He says "Lydia?"
    Lydia says "Robert."
    Robert says "Are you alright?"
    Lydia says "No. I don't know."
    Robert says "What?" He says "What?"
    Lydia says "Anthony's..." Lydia is crying. "I don't know. It's a long story. I just wanted to hear your voice." Lydia says "Yeah. Yeah, no that's all. I'm drunk, I don't know. I'm sorry. I just think about you. I don't know. Like, I know you're... I don't know." She says "I'm sorry." Robert's eyes open and close. His upper lip moves up and down. Robert makes a quick, small sound. Lydia says "What?"

Robert is lying on his bed. He is touching his cat. Robert thinks "I want to call Kelly." Robert thinks "Kelly is sitting in her house with Abby." He thinks "Kelly and Abby are dipping something into hummus. They're listening to Feist." Robert looks at his cell phone. Robert touches his cell phone. He stands up. Robert's cat makes a sound. Robert walks to the kitchen. He drinks a glass of water. He washes the glass. He looks at his cell phone. He walks outside. It's sunny. Robert touches his arm. His arm is warm. Robert walks inside. Robert looks at his bookcase. Robert walks into his bedroom. He sits in a chair. Robert checks his email. He has no new email. Robert opens iTunes. Robert plays the song "The Orchids" by Psychic TV. Robert thinks "I want to be outside. I want to go on a bike ride." Robert looks at his cell phone. He plugs his cell phone into its charger. Robert takes a shower. Robert dries himself. He puts on underwear. He puts on jeans. He puts on a t-shirt. He takes off the t-shirt. He puts the t-shirt back on. He puts on socks and shoes. He looks at himself in the mirror. He looks at his laptop computer. He looks at his cat. Robert walks out of his apartment. He walks down stairs. He walks out of his building. Robert rides his bike. He is in front of a cafe. People are sitting outside the cafe. Robert rides his bike. He is in front of a movie theater. He looks at the marquee. He rides his bike. He is in front of his building. He walks into his building. He walks up stairs. He walks into his apartment. Robert plays the album *Beggars Banquet* by The Rolling Stones. He lies on the couch. He thinks "There's a party or something tonight. It's okay to do what I'm doing." He thinks "I shouldn't worry so much, or like I don't have to, at least."

Robert is awake. He thinks "I have today off and I have tomorrow off." He stands up. He sits in a chair. He opens iTunes. He plays the song "Hustlin'" by Rick Ross. He thinks "I'm better than Rick Ross." Robert walks outside. It's cold. He walks inside. Robert makes tofu scramble. He makes home fries. He puts tofu scramble and home fries on a plate. He puts ketchup on the plate. He thinks "Organic ketchup." He thinks "It doesn't matter what I do." He pours water into a glass. He puts the plate and the glass on the kitchen table. He tears a paper towel from a roll of paper towels. He puts the paper towel on the kitchen table. Robert sits on a chair. He eats. He drinks. He thinks "This is good." Robert rubs the paper towel against his mouth. He throws out the paper towel. Robert puts the frying pan into the sink. He puts water in the frying pan. He puts dish soap in the frying pan. He puts the plate on top of the frying pan. He puts the glass into the sink. Robert walks into his bedroom. He looks at his cell phone. Robert sits in the chair near his laptop computer. He opens iTunes. Robert plays the album *The Magic of Satie* by Jean-Yves Thibaudet. He walks into the bathroom. Robert takes a shower. He walks into his bedroom. Robert puts on jeans. He looks at himself in the mirror. He puts on a t-shirt. He puts on shoes. Robert walks into the kitchen. He sweeps the kitchen floor. Robert walks into his bedroom. He makes his bed. Robert lies on his bed. He plays the album *The Adventures of Ghosthorse and Stillborn* by CocoRosie. Robert thinks "I want to sleep for the rest of the day." He thinks "I want to sleep for the rest of my life. I don't know."

Robert is standing on a subway platform. Kelly, Abby, Steve and Ted are there. Robert, Kelly, Abby, Steve and Ted are each holding a grocery bag from Trader Joe's. Robert thinks "I'm the only person in the world. More than ever, there is only me." A train comes. Robert, Kelly, Abby, Steve and Ted walk onto the train. Robert, Kelly, Steve and Ted stand on the train. Abby sits down. Robert says "Lil Wayne is the greatest rapper of all time." Robert, Kelly, Abby, Steve and Ted get off the train. They walk to Kelly and Abby's house. They walk into Kelly and Abby's house. They walk into the kitchen. They put the grocery bags on the kitchen table. Abby, Steve and Ted leave the kitchen.

Kelly says "Do you want tea?" Robert looks at Kelly.

Robert says "Yeah." Robert looks at the grocery bags. Robert says "Thank you." He walks to Kelly. He touches her hair. Kelly looks at Robert. She touches his side. Robert says "I have to go wash my hands." Robert walks to the bathroom. Robert thinks "I do not want to leave the bathroom." There are no magazines in the bathroom. Robert washes his hands. The song "Our Faces Split The Coast In Half" by Broken Social Scene is playing. Robert walks into the kitchen. He looks at Kelly.

A man says "Everything, right down to the ice cubes in your iced soy latte there, is made with filtered water."

Robert says "Thank you." He looks at his iced soy latte. Robert says "Is there an internet password?" The man rips a receipt off of the cash register. He highlights a line of text.

The man says "Here you go." He hands Robert the receipt.

Robert says "Thanks." Robert sits down. He drinks iced soy latte. He takes the case for his laptop computer out of his book bag. He takes his laptop computer out of its case. He places his laptop computer on the table. Robert puts the case for his laptop computer into his book bag. Robert opens his laptop computer. He turns on his laptop computer. Robert checks his email. He doesn't have any new email. Robert thinks "I wish MySpace and Facebook wouldn't email me when people send me messages or leave comments or anything, so I would have another website to log on to. As it is, I know that nothing new is happening on MySpace or Facebook." He thinks "There's probably an option for that." Robert takes the lid off of his iced soy latte container. He drinks iced soy latte.

Robert, Jim and Tom smoke pot. Robert and Tom walk outside. They ride bikes. Robert thinks "This area reminds me of an area near where I grew up." Robert thinks "I long for a carefree time." Robert says "Ay." Tom looks at Robert.

Tom says "What's up dude?" Robert is high. They are in a neighborhood west of Robert's neighborhood. Robert thinks "These houses are nice."

Robert says "We should just move into one of these houses, dude."

Tom says "Yeah." He laughs.

Robert says "How much do you think they go for?"

Tom says "I bet nothing around here ever goes on the market because the same Italian families have lived in them for the past hundred and fifty years."

Robert says "It would be totally sweet to live in one of these houses though. A yard and shit. No trash on the ground." A Chevy Caprice drives past Robert and Tom. The song "Put Some Keys On That" by Lil Wayne is playing in the Chevrolet Caprice. Robert says "Yo that's my joint yo."

Tom says "Yeah okay." Robert and Tom ride bikes. There is a red light. Tom says "Moving out here wouldn't change anything. You wouldn't be doing anything different, you'd just live in a nicer place."

Robert says "No yeah I know. Yeah. I don't know."

Robert is sitting down. The song "Don't Talk (Put Your Head On My Shoulder)" by The Beach Boys is playing. Robert looks out the window. Robert's hair is wet. He sees someone approach a building across the street. Robert thinks "I have to go to work soon." Robert looks at the person across the street. Robert looks at his own hands. Robert looks at his laptop computer. He looks at the track listing for the album *Pet Sounds* by The Beach Boys. He looks at a door open across the street. Robert sees someone step outside. The two people across the street are talking. Robert doesn't hear what they are saying. Robert thinks "I want someone to talk to me." Robert walks to the kitchen. He makes a peanut butter and jelly sandwich.

It's night. Robert and Tom walk past a beer store. Robert looks at it. He looks at Tom. Robert and Tom talk. They walk past a beer store. Robert doesn't look at it. Robert and Tom are in front of Robert's building. They look at the sky. They talk. They walk inside. They walk up stairs. They walk into Robert's apartment. Robert and Tom sit on the couch. They watch *Chungking Express*. Tom says "This is really bad."

Robert says "Yeah." *Chungking Express* starts to skip a lot. Robert turns off the TV. Robert turns off the DVD player. Robert and Tom talk. They walk into Robert's room. Robert puts a blanket on the floor. He puts a pillow on the floor. Tom lies on the blanket on the floor. Robert lies on his bed. They are asleep. They are awake. Robert stands up. Tom stands up. They walk to the kitchen. Robert says "Do you want coffee?"

Tom says "No, I think I'm going to sleep more when I get home." Robert and Tom walk out of Robert's apartment. They walk down stairs. They walk outside. Robert and Tom walk to a subway station. Tom walks into the subway station. Robert walks. Robert buys two pieces of tomato pie. He eats the tomato pie. Robert is sweating. He walks to his building. He walks up stairs. He walks into his apartment. He walks into his bedroom. Robert lies on his bed. He reads the story "Soldier's Home" by Ernest Hemingway. Robert is asleep. He is awake. Robert calls Alison.

Alison says "Hi."

Robert says "Are you sleeping?"

Alison says "I'm trying not to—I'm at the library reading about economics, well actually it's history."

Robert says "Okay, well don't sleep then. I'll talk to you later."

Alison says "Well, what's going on?"

Robert says "Nothing. I just wanted to chitchat. But if you're in the library you shouldn't be chitchatting. Goodnight."

Alison says "Goodnight." Robert turns on his bedside lamp. He takes out his contact lenses. Robert turns off his bedside lamp.

Robert walks into his building. He opens his mailbox. He looks in his mailbox. Robert picks up an envelope from Netflix. He closes his mailbox. Robert walks up stairs. He walks into his apartment. He opens the envelope from Netflix. He reads a description of the movie *The Squid and the Whale*. Robert walks to his bedroom. He takes off his clothes. Robert plays the album *Lambent Material* by Eluvium. He lies on his bed. His eyes are closed. Robert stands up. He puts on shorts. He walks to the kitchen. He looks at the window. He pours water into a glass. He looks at his cat. He thinks "I wish I was at my parents' house." Robert thinks "What's going on tonight? Should I call someone?" Robert calls Kelly. He leaves a voicemail. Robert thinks "I'm not sure what to do." Robert opens the freezer. He picks up an ice cube tray. Robert walks to his bedroom. He lies on his bed. Robert takes an ice cube out of the ice cube tray. He places the ice cube on his stomach.

The song "Nothing But Flowers" by Talking Heads is playing. Robert feels oil move on his face. There is a noise. Robert walks into the bathroom. He washes his face. He walks into his bedroom. He picks up a shirt off the floor. He puts it on a hanger. He puts it in the closet. He thinks "I'm glad I don't have work tomorrow." Robert looks at his cell phone. He thinks "I haven't accomplished anything." He thinks "I'm still young though." Robert plays the album *Paper Television* by The Blow. He thinks "The Blow's percussion is good." Robert calls Kelly. He leaves a voicemail. It's eight fifty-five p.m. Robert looks at his wireless modem. He looks at his cat. Robert thinks "Did I do something wrong in raising my cat? I jumped into cat ownership, I guess." He feels oil move on his face. He thinks "I guess I should eat better." Robert takes a shower. He calls Kelly. He doesn't leave a voicemail. He thinks "What is everyone doing?" He thinks "What are my Spanish-speaking neighbors doing?" There is a noise. Robert looks at his cat. Robert's cat vomits. Robert looks at it. Robert walks to the bathroom. Robert picks up toilet paper. He puts some of the toilet paper under running water. Robert carries the dry toilet paper and the wet toilet paper to his bedroom. He rubs the wet toilet paper against the floor. He rubs the dry toilet paper against the floor. Robert walks to the bathroom. He drops the toilet paper into the toilet. He washes his hands. Robert brushes his teeth. He takes out his contact lenses. Robert walks to his bedroom. He looks at his cat. He thinks "I should exercise more. I hardly exercise."

Robert and Kelly are sitting on a bench. It's warm. Robert looks at Kelly. Robert thinks "Kissing Kelly feels good. Kissing Kelly would feel good." Robert looks at Kelly. Robert says "I don't think we can really... Um... I don't... There isn't any chance that we can ever be boyfriend and girlfriend so I don't think we should really pursue this any further." Kelly's facial expression changes. Robert says "I really like you though and I think you're really great and I really did have a really great time tonight." He says "I'm sorry."

Kelly says "Wow." Kelly says "Wow, I just really... Well you have to tell me why, because, wow, I just really, thought, well, I just... well what you said. I thought we were really pretty great together. Like pretty... whatever."

Robert says "Yeah." He says "Yeah." He says "Yeah, it's just..." Robert thinks "I don't like her clothes and I don't think she's—I don't want to introduce her to my friends, the ones that I don't have yet but who will be more like me, vain and judgmental and stuff." He thinks "I need to stop being like this." He thinks "Run into traffic." He thinks "It's not going fast enough to kill me probably."

Robert is in Borders. He looks at the new issue of *The Paris Review*. Robert stands on an escalator. He is on the second floor. Robert looks at the book *The Easter Parade* by Richard Yates. The album *Challengers* by The New Pornographers is playing in Borders. Robert thinks "Can I talk to one of the girls that works here? Probably not, right? Of course not." Robert is near the escalator. He looks at a young woman. He thinks "I'm going to talk to that girl.

I'm just going to say something, because I have to talk
to someone." A Mexican man is standing behind Robert.
Robert thinks "I need to go down the escalator." Robert
stands on the escalator. He is on the first floor. Robert
walks outside. He walks into a grocery store. He looks
at a large bag of organic corn chips. It costs three dollars
and forty-nine cents. He walks outside. Robert walks into
a grocery store. He looks at a small bag of organic pretzels. It costs one dollar and ninety-nine cents. He walks
outside. He looks at a guitar store. He walks into Whole
Foods. He looks at a small bag of organic vegetable chips.
It costs seventy-nine cents. He buys a five-pound bag of
organic russet potatoes. It costs three dollars and ninety-
nine cents. Robert walks outside. He is walking. Robert
sees Dan. Dan is riding a bike. Robert says "Hey Dan."
Dan says "Hey Robert. What's up man?"

Robert says "I don't know. What are you doing?"

Dan says "Just going to the beer store."

Robert says "Oh yeah? You're drinking beer tonight?"
Robert smiles. Dan smiles.

Dan says "I drink beer every night pretty much." Dan
says "So yeah."

Robert says "I was just going to head over to your place
and see if you guys were drinking beer."

Dan says "I could uh pick something up for you, though
I'm already picking up...well, yeah I guess I probably could."

Robert says "That would be great." Robert takes a five-
dollar bill from his pocket. He says, "Could you get me a
forty of O.E.?"

Dan says "Yeah alright." Robert hands Dan the five-dollar bill. Dan says "I guess I'll see you over there then."

Robert says "Thanks man." Robert walks to Dan's house. He walks inside. Rachel, Ted and Ashley are there. Robert thinks "They're happy to see me." He thinks "Dan was happy to see me." Everyone talks. Dan walks inside.

Dan says "Robert, I'm sorry man, no forties of O.E., I got you two twenty-four-ounce cans." Dan hands Robert two twenty-four-ounce cans of Olde English malt liquor. He hands Robert a one-dollar bill.

Robert says "No that's good. That's so good. Thank you." Robert puts a twenty-four-ounce can of Olde English malt liquor in the refrigerator. He opens a twenty-four-ounce can of Olde English malt liquor. Robert drinks Olde English malt liquor. Robert and Rachel make french fries. Everyone eats french fries. Everyone walks outside. Everyone talks. Everyone smokes cigarettes. Robert and Dan ride bikes to a pretzel factory. They buy pretzels. They ride bikes to a beer store. They buy beer. Robert and Dan ride bikes to Dan's house. They walk inside. Dan walks up stairs. Robert walks to the kitchen. He opens the refrigerator. He picks up a twenty-four-ounce can of Olde English malt liquor. Robert closes the refrigerator. Robert walks up stairs. He walks into Dan's bedroom. Everyone is in Dan's bedroom. Robert opens the can of Olde English malt liquor. He drinks Olde English malt liquor. Robert makes faces at Rachel. Rachel makes faces at Robert. Robert thinks "I have no idea how Rachel feels about me." Robert is asleep. He is awake.

Robert is lying on a small burgundy couch. Robert stands up. He looks at his jeans. There is mustard on Robert's jeans. He looks at his shoes. There is mustard on Robert's left shoe. Robert thinks "I feel okay." He looks at his cell phone. It's six fifteen a.m. Robert walks into the bathroom. He washes his hands. He washes his face. He looks at the mustard on his clothes. He thinks "Um." Robert walks to the front door. He unlocks the front door. He opens the front door. Robert walks outside. He turns the lock. He closes the door. Robert thinks "Did I lock the door?" He opens the door. He thinks "Um." He thinks "Should I try to lock the door more?" He turns the lock. He closes the door. Robert walks away. Ted opens the door. Ted looks at Robert. Robert looks at the mustard on his clothes. He looks at Ted.

Ted says "Oh, later man."

Robert says "Bye." He thinks "I feel like I'm wearing headphones or something." He walks to his building. There are people outside. Robert thinks "I like to see people walking in the morning." Robert thinks "I'm thirsty." Robert walks into his building. He walks up stairs. He walks into his apartment.

Jim says "Hey Rob." Jim is lying on the couch. Jim says "Just get back from partying?"

Robert says "Yeah I was over at Dan and Ted's."

Jim says "Oh, you were over there?"

Robert says "Yeah." Robert pours water into a glass. He drinks the water. He pours water into the glass. He drinks the water. Robert puts the glass into the sink. He says "I'm going to bed." He walks to his bedroom. He takes off his clothes. Robert lies on his bed. He plays the album *The Ramones* by The Ramones. He picks up the book *Then We Came To The End* by Joshua Ferris. He reads the first twenty pages of *Then We Came To The End*. Robert thinks "Should I go back to sleep?" He walks to his laptop computer. Robert looks at Facebook. He changes his Facebook status to "Robert is I just woke up and I'm not sure whether or not I should go back to sleep. PS: I'm drunk." Robert walks into the bathroom. He washes his face. He washes his hands. Robert walks into his bedroom. He lies on his bed. Robert is asleep.

Robert is lying on his bed. He looks at his alarm clock. It's ten fifty a.m. Robert thinks "I don't have work today or tomorrow." He thinks "I want to go back to sleep." Robert closes his eyes. He opens his eyes. Robert looks at his alarm clock. It's eleven twenty-eight a.m. Robert thinks "When I told Kelly that we could never be boyfriend and girlfriend or something I felt one feeling. Now I feel another feeling. Or the same feeling. I feel something right now." Robert thinks "I should make spaghetti." Robert plays the song "December, 1963 (Oh What a Night)" by Frankie Valli and the Four Seasons. Robert stands up. He walks into the bathroom. He washes his face. He pees. Robert washes his hands. He thinks "I should take a shower." Robert walks into his bedroom. He closes the curtains. He thinks "I wish it were darker." He takes off his clothes. He lies on his bed. He stands up. Robert takes all the sheets off his bed. He lies on his bed. He turns off his bedside lamp. He looks out the window.

Robert is lying on the couch. *Late Night with Conan O'Brien* is on TV. Robert is looking at the TV. Robert isn't wearing a shirt. He is eating spaghetti. His legs are sweating. Outside, someone yells. Robert thinks "There is acne on my face." Robert turns off the TV. He pours water into a glass. He walks into his bedroom. He checks his email. Robert has an email from his mother. He looks at himself in the mirror. He walks into the bathroom. He washes his face. He thinks "Shower." He looks at the book *The Selected Letters of James Thurber*. He thinks "When am I going to read *The Selected Letters of James Thurber*?" He thinks "Should I put *The Selected Letters of James Thurber* on eBay? It looks impressive, kind of." Robert takes a shower. He walks into his bedroom. He takes the sheets off his bed. He lies on his bed. There is a tennis shirt, two socks, two collared shirts, and one pair of jeans on Robert's bedroom floor. Robert thinks "Would I be happier if those things were put away?" Robert walks to his laptop computer. He checks his email. He has no new email. He plays the song "Forever For Her (Is Over For Me)" by The White Stripes. He lies on his bed. He thinks "Smoking pot would make me feel a little better." He thinks "Or no, I'd probably just breathe weird and fall asleep." Robert stands up. He turns off his overhead light.

He lies on his bed. Robert thinks "I wish I had glow-in-the-dark star stickers on my ceiling. Sometimes people put those stickers on their ceiling fans and it looks really cool." Robert looks out the window. He takes off his jeans. He takes off his socks. He walks into the bathroom. He brushes his teeth. He walks into his bedroom. He lies on his bed.

Robert is riding his bike. He's wearing a sweater. There is a red light. Robert stops riding his bike. He looks at a flower shop. His eyes are wet. Robert touches his eyes. The light turns green. Robert starts riding his bike. He thinks "Should I go to Whole Foods?"

Robert is walking. It's warm. Robert thinks "Should I get coffee or something?" Robert sees an art gallery. He looks at the art gallery. He opens the door to the art gallery. Robert walks into the art gallery. There is an old man in the art gallery. Robert nods at the old man. Robert looks at water-color paintings. Robert looks at three young women. One of the young women is looking at a laptop computer. Robert walks into another part of the gallery. He looks at three photographs of someone wearing underpants. The view in all three photographs is from the waist down. Robert looks at a jar of red dust. The jar is labeled "tight jeans."

Robert opens his curtains. He opens the window. He looks out the window. Middle Eastern children are playing in the street. Robert looks at the Middle Eastern children. Robert sits down. He types "when i make bank deposits i sometimes write your phone number instead of my account number by accident." Robert highlights the text. He presses delete.

Robert is walking. He looks at a building. He thinks "Would I be happier if I lived in that building?" Robert walks into the building where he works. He checks his email. Robert walks outside. He looks at a young woman. She is carrying a tote bag. The young woman's tote bag says "Suicide Squeeze Records." The young woman has black hair. Robert says "Hi." Robert looks at the young woman. The young woman looks at Robert. The young woman walks away. Robert walks into the building where he works.

Robert walks into his building. He walks up stairs. He walks into his apartment. Robert lies on the couch. He closes his eyes. He thinks "Email." He walks into his bedroom. He sits near his laptop computer. He plays the album *You Forgot It In People* by Broken Social Scene. He lies on his bed. He looks out the window. Robert looks at the sky. He looks at the tops of buildings across the street. He thinks "I am listening to Broken Social Scene. I feel a little better than I would otherwise because I am listening to Broken Social Scene." He thinks "I'm tired." He thinks "Email." Robert walks into the kitchen. He pours water into a glass. He sits on the couch. He pets his cat. He thinks "Is the video store still open?" He walks to his bedroom. He plays the song "Shimmy Shimmy Ya" by Ol' Dirty Bastard. He checks his email. He has four new emails. He reads his email. He writes an email. He walks to the kitchen. He opens the refrigerator. He looks at the refrigerator. He looks at eggs. He touches them. Robert walks out of his apartment. He walks down stairs. He walks out of his building. Robert sits on the stoop. He thinks "I wish I had cigarettes or something." He thinks "I remember smoking cigarettes." He thinks "I should only do positive things." Robert walks into his building. He walks up stairs. He walks into his apartment. Robert picks up money. He puts money into his pocket. Robert walks outside. Robert walks to Pathmark. He walks into Pathmark. Robert is walking. Robert thinks "I like the way peppermint candy, religious candles and tomato paste packaging look." Robert walks towards the exit. He sees a product called Organic Fruit Roll. Robert picks up an Organic Fruit Roll. He walks to the automated check out line. Robert pays a dollar and twenty-nine cents for the Organic Fruit Roll. A young woman wearing a Pathmark uniform says "Have a good night."

Robert says "You too." Robert is outside. He thinks "Is there something I should do?" Robert walks to his building. He thinks "I wonder what it's like to work at Pathmark. Should I get a job at Pathmark?" He thinks "I like my job I guess." Robert walks into his building. He walks up stairs. He walks into his apartment. Robert opens the refrigerator door. He puts the Organic Fruit Roll in the refrigerator. He closes the refrigerator door. He opens the refrigerator door. He looks at the Organic Fruit Roll. He looks at Organic

Rice Drink. Robert picks up Organic Rice Drink. He pours
Organic Rice Drink into a glass. He puts Organic Rice Drink
into the refrigerator. Robert looks at Organic Fruit Roll. He
closes the refrigerator door. He drinks Organic Rice Drink.
He puts the glass into the sink. He walks to the bathroom.
He brushes his teeth. He washes his face. Robert walks into
his bedroom. He checks his email. He has no new email.
Robert plays the album *A Certain Smile, A Certain Sadness*
by Rocketship. He lies on his bed. He looks out the window.
The sky is black. The buildings across the street are gray.
Robert thinks "Like probably down the hall or next door or
across the street there's a girl I've never met who is thinking
exactly the same things as me. We're never going to meet,
we're both just going to I don't know."

Robert takes a shower. He walks into his bedroom. He puts
on clothes. He walks to the kitchen. He washes dishes. He
thinks "I'm always happy when I get drunk and don't fuck
things up too bad. I always think, 'That was dumb. I'm fine.'"
Robert lies on the couch. He stands up. He looks at a pile of
DVDs. He picks up a DVD. The DVD is *Lost in Translation*.
Robert turns on the DVD player. He puts *Lost in Translation*
into the DVD player. Robert turns on the TV. He presses
play. Robert lies on the couch. He thinks "I should stop eating
wheat maybe." Robert thinks "Bill Murray."

Robert is at a used clothing store. Robert is holding a sweater. He is standing in a line. There is one person in front of

Robert in the line. Robert looks at the person in front of him. He looks at the salesperson. Robert takes a twenty-dollar bill out of his pocket. The person in front of Robert leaves. Robert puts the sweater on the counter. The salesperson looks at the sweater. The salesperson says "It's sixteen dollars and fifty cents." Robert hands the salesperson the twenty-dollar bill. The salesperson says "Out of twenty?"

Robert says "Yeah." The salesperson does something with the twenty-dollar bill. Robert says "I don't need a bag." Robert puts the sweater into his book bag. The salesperson hands Robert three one-dollar bills, two quarters, and a receipt. Robert puts his change and the receipt into his pocket. He says "Thank you." Robert walks outside. It's cold. Robert takes the sweater out of his book bag. He puts on the sweater. Robert thinks "Are people watching me?" Robert thinks "Would I watch someone on the street put on a sweater?" He thinks "Why haven't I asked myself that before?"

It's Friday. Robert brushes his teeth. He thinks "I'm healthy." He thinks, "Should I have a bigger medicine cabinet? At my parents' house the medicine cabinet is bigger. They have so much stuff in their medicine cabinet. I should have more stuff. At some point." Robert walks into the kitchen. His cat is on top of the refrigerator. Robert says "Come on, baby." He picks up his cat. Robert's cat scratches Robert's hand. Robert walks into his bedroom. He closes the door. Robert puts down his cat. His cat lies on the floor. Robert lies on his bed. "Addicted to Love" by Ciccone Youth is playing. Robert's cat jumps on Robert's bed. Robert looks at his cat. His cat is licking itself. Robert puts his forefinger near where his cat is licking itself. Robert thinks "Security."

Robert is awake. His mouth is dry. His bedside light is on. Robert looks at his alarm clock. It's three a.m. Robert is wearing jeans and socks. Robert walks into the living room. The lights are on. The TV is on. The TV shows the DVD player's screensaver. Jim is lying on the couch. Jim is asleep. There is a black plastic bag next to the couch. Robert's cat is lying on the floor. Robert's cat is next to the black plastic bag. There are two twenty-four-ounce cans of Ice House beer next to the black plastic bag. Robert pours water into a glass. He drinks water. Robert pours water into the glass. He drinks water. Robert puts the glass into the sink. Robert thinks "I hope my mouth isn't always dry." Robert walks into his bedroom. He sits near his laptop computer. He checks his email. He has no new email. Robert thinks "I wish I had new email." Robert looks at a bag of cashews. He thinks "What should I do?" He thinks "Will eating cashews make my mouth more dry?" He thinks "Should I take off my socks?"

Robert is riding his bike. He touches the back of his jeans. He thinks "Where's my wallet?" Robert stops riding his bike. He thinks "Where is my wallet?" Robert touches the front of his jeans. He touches his jacket. Robert rides his bike slowly. He looks at the ground. Robert thinks "It feels good to ride slow, kind of." Robert rides his bike to his building. He walks into his building. He walks up stairs. Robert walks into his apartment. He walks into his bedroom. Robert sits next to his laptop computer. He looks at his laptop computer. He looks at his bank's website. Robert takes his cell phone out of his pocket. He thinks "At least I didn't lose my cell phone. I guess that would have been better, though." Robert calls his bank's twenty-four-hour help line. He talks to an operator. Robert is on hold. He talks to an operator. Robert has his debit card put on hold. The operator says "Can I help you with anything else?"

Robert says "No, you've been very helpful, thank you."

The operator says "Thank you. Have a good night." Robert thinks "That was easy." He checks his email. Robert has two new emails. It's seven forty-five p.m. Robert puts on clothes. It's eight thirty-five. Robert walks into the living room. He picks up a bottle of wine. He puts the bottle of wine into a bag. He walks out of his apartment. He walks down stairs. He walks outside. It's cold. Robert walks to Karen's apartment. He calls Karen. Karen walks outside. She says "Hi Robert."

Robert says "Hi Karen." Robert and Karen hug. Robert and Karen walk into Karen's building. They walk up stairs. Robert and Karen walk into Karen's apartment. There are people in Karen's apartment. Robert says something about a corkscrew. Karen opens a drawer. She closes the drawer. She opens a drawer.

Karen says "I don't think I have a corkscrew."

Robert says "Oh, that's okay." He puts the bottle of wine on the kitchen counter. Robert thinks "Why did I bring wine?" Robert drinks beer. Someone does something with a hammer and a screwdriver. The wine bottle is open. Robert says "Thank you." Robert offers people wine. Robert pours wine into a glass. Robert has wine on his shirt. Someone hands Robert an ice cube. Robert says "Thank you." He thinks "I want to go home. I shouldn't have brought a bottle of wine. I have to go to work tomorrow." Karen touches Robert's shoulder. Robert looks at Karen.

Karen says "Do you want to smoke pot?"

Robert says "Uh. Yeah." Robert and Karen walk into Karen's bedroom. There are people in Karen's bedroom. Karen closes the door. People smoke pot. Karen smokes pot. Robert smokes pot. Robert leans close to people. He whispers jokes to people. Karen touches Robert's shoulder. Robert looks at Karen.

Karen says "I just want you to know that I know that you're full of bullshit."

Robert says "That makes me feel sad."

Karen says "What?"

Robert says "I know I project that sometimes, that full of shit thing, but inside I'm really deep." He thinks "I am fucked up right now."

Karen says "Yeah, and that's why you're full of bullshit."

Robert says "Oh." He says "Okay." Robert thinks, "She's drunk, I guess. I guess that's fine." Robert walks into the living room. He picks up a carrot. Robert dips the carrot into ranch dip. He thinks "Fuck." He eats the carrot. A young woman walks towards Robert.

The young woman says "Borges. I thought about it. Borges." The young woman walks away.

Robert says "I need to puke." A young man holds Robert's hand. Robert and the young man walk. Robert walks into the bathroom. Robert looks at the sink. He looks at the toilet. Robert thinks "What the fuck?" Robert thinks "Fuck." Robert walks into the living room. He looks at people. He throws up. Karen holds Robert's hand. She walks to the bathroom. Robert walks to the bathroom. He splashes water onto his face. Karen hands Robert a towel. Robert rubs the towel against his face.

Karen says "Here, rinse your mouth out." Robert cups his hands under the faucet. He puts water in his mouth. He spits water into the sink. There are chunks of vomit in the sink. Robert looks at the chunks of vomit. He looks at Karen. Karen is frowning. Robert rubs the towel against his face. Robert hands Karen the towel. She drops it on the floor. Robert and Karen leave the bathroom. Robert looks at people. Robert and Karen walk outside. They walk toward Robert's building. They stop walking.

Robert says "I've got it from here." He says "Thank you, Karen." He says "I'm so sorry." Karen looks at Robert. She looks at his shoes. Robert looks at his shoes. There is vomit on Robert's shoes. There is vomit on Robert's vest. Robert touches his vest.

Karen says "It's, no, it's so, it's okay. I'm sorry." She says "You'll be okay walking home?"

Robert says "Yeah. You shouldn't walk home from my apartment. I'm okay." Karen looks at Robert. She bites her lip.

Karen says "You're just so drunk." Robert walks to his building. He walks into his building. He walks up stairs. He walks into his apartment. He walks into his bedroom. Robert takes off his clothes. He takes all the sheets off of his bed. Robert lies on his bed. It's three a.m. Robert plays the song "Paper Planes" by M.I.A. Robert is asleep. Robert is awake. It's seven a.m. Robert thinks "I'll get up at eight." He sets his alarm clock for eight a.m. He sets his cell phone alarm for eight-thirty a.m. Robert is asleep. Robert is awake. He walks to the bathroom. He pees. He looks at himself in the mirror. He walks into his bedroom. He checks his email. He has three new emails. He plays the song "Paper Planes" by M.I.A. He thinks "I'll still be pretty efficient at work."

Robert is awake. There are keys in Robert's pocket. Robert stands up. He puts on shoes. He puts on glasses. Robert walks into the living room. He looks at his cat. He says "Hi baby." Robert walks out of his apartment. He walks down stairs. He walks outside. It's sunny. Robert is walking. He walks past Spanish-speaking teenagers. He walks into a laundromat. Robert opens a washing machine. He closes the washing machine. Robert opens a washing machine. Robert takes clothing out of the washing machine. He closes the washing machine. Robert opens a dryer. He puts the clothing into the dryer. He closes the dryer. He puts quarters into the dryer. He presses a button. He thinks "I should have used fabric softener. I have that fabric softener, I should use it." He walks outside. He is walking. He walks past Spanish-speaking teenagers. Robert walks into his building. He walks up stairs. He walks into his apartment. He walks into his bedroom. He looks at his laptop computer. He plays the album *Blonde on Blonde* by Bob Dylan. He lies down. He sits up. He opens the window. Robert lights a cigarette. He smokes a cigarette. He puts the cigarette out on the window-sill. He thinks "My life is okay." It's warm. *Blonde on Blonde* ends. Robert stands up. He picks up a laundry bag. He walks out of his apartment. He walks down stairs. He walks outside. He walks to the laundromat. He walks into the laundromat. Robert opens the dryer. He takes clothing out of the dryer. He puts the clothing into the laundry bag. Robert closes the dryer. He walks outside. He walks to his building. He walks into his building. Robert walks up stairs. He walks into his apartment. He puts the laundry bag on the floor. Robert sits on the couch. He looks at his cat. Robert touches his cat. Robert takes clothing out of the laundry bag. He puts clothing on the coffee table. Robert folds clothing. He stands up. He stands near the stereo. He plays "Piano Sonata No. 14 (Moonlight)" by Beethoven on the stereo. Robert walks into the kitchen. He looks out the window.

Robert looks at his laptop computer. He masturbates. Robert thinks "I wish I had a girlfriend. Is what I'm doing right now lowering my chances of having a girlfriend?" Robert looks at his laptop computer. He ejaculates. He collects the semen with his hand. He thinks "Do I have to put on clothes to walk to the bathroom?" He puts on underpants. Robert walks to the bathroom. He holds his towel with one hand and his semen with the other hand. Robert is in the bathroom. He turns on the shower. He puts the towel on the toilet. He puts his semen-covered hand under the water. Robert rubs his non-semen-covered hand against his semen-covered hand. The water becomes warm. Robert stands in the shower. He washes himself.

Robert is in front of his building. He is leaning on an SUV. Jim is next to Robert. Jim is leaning on the SUV. Dan and Ashley are sitting on the stoop. Everyone smokes a cigarette. Robert, Jim and Dan hold cans of Pabst Blue Ribbon beer. Ashley holds a glass of Bacardi rum and Coke. Dan and Ashley are talking. Jim says "R-Man, I really like being your roommate." Robert thinks "I wish Jim wasn't drunk already. It's still light out."

Robert says "Well I like being your roommate, Jim."

Jim say "I know you don't like me too much, but—"

Robert says "I like you, Jim."

Jim says "I know you don't, but it's okay." He drinks from his can of Pabst Blue Ribbon beer. Robert drinks from his can of Pabst Blue Ribbon beer. Jim says "But I really do like you. I think you're a stand-up guy." He drinks from his can of Pabst Blue Ribbon beer. He says "I know I'm just a dunce." Robert shakes his head. Jim says "No, I know."

Robert touches Jim's back. Robert looks at Jim. Jim looks at the ground.

Robert says "No, Jim. I like you." Robert looks at Dan and Ashley. Dan and Ashley look at Robert and Jim. Jim looks at the ground. He smiles. Jim looks at Dan and Ashley. Everyone walks into Robert's building. They walk up stairs. They walk into Robert's apartment. Robert plays the album *Only Built 4 Cuban Linx* by Raekwon. Everyone sits on chairs. They drink. They play cards. Dan and Ashley leave. Robert and Jim sit on the couch. They drink water. Robert says "Goodnight Jim."

Jim says "Goodnight."

Robert opens a can of organic vegetable soup. He puts the soup into a pot. He turns the stove on. Robert looks at the pot. Robert pours orange juice into a glass. Robert drinks the orange juice. He walks to the window. He looks at the park across the street. Robert thinks "I don't have work tomorrow." It's nine p.m. It is warm. Robert looks at the soup. He tastes the soup. He turns the stove off. He pours the soup into a bowl. He takes the bowl to the kitchen table. Robert eats the soup. He thinks "This is salty." Robert looks at an issue of *Granta*. Robert reads a story by Saul Bellow. He walks to his bedroom. Robert takes his contact lenses out. He lies on his bed. Robert thinks "I want there to be a girl, and for it to be realistic. I want to live with a girl. We would make food together and then we would eat food together. We would do dishes. I would do dishes and she would put things away. We'd lie in bed. What would I think about?"

Robert is sitting down. He is in his parents' house. He is in the living room. Robert is watching *The Office*. He is eating corn chips and salsa. Robert's father is sitting near Robert. Robert's father is looking at a paperback book. A commercial comes on. Robert picks up the remote. He presses the mute button. Robert says "I'm gonna go out, I think."

Robert's father says "Poker game?"

Robert says "No, I'm hanging out with Lydia."

Robert's father says "Have fun."

Robert says "I'll try." Robert walks to the kitchen. He puts the corn chips on the counter. He puts the salsa in the refrigerator. He puts on shoes. He puts a key ring in his pocket. Robert walks outside. He gets into his car. Robert's mother's car pulls into the driveway. Robert looks at his mother's car. Robert's mother gets out of her car. Robert gets out of his car. Robert and his mother talk.

Robert's mother says "Where are you going?"

Robert says "I'm going over to Lydia's."

Robert's mother says "Well, have fun. You going to be late?"

Robert says "I'm not sure. Probably not."

Robert's mother says "Well, have fun. Be careful."

Robert says "Thanks. See ya." Robert gets into his car.

Robert's mother walks into Robert's parents' house. Robert looks at his mother. He looks at his parents' house. Robert pulls out of the driveway. He plays the album *Pop The Glock* by Uffie. He thinks "I'm healthy." Robert drives over a small bridge. He thinks "Lydia." He turns up the volume. Robert drives to Lydia's parents' house. Robert calls Lydia.

Lydia says "Hello?"

Robert says "I'm here."

Lydia says "Come in. It's open." Robert walks into Lydia's parents' house. Robert walks to the kitchen. Lydia is making falafel. Robert looks at Lydia. Robert thinks "If I spent more time with Lydia I would be more depressed I think. She is a little hot. No. I don't know." He thinks "She isn't hot enough." Robert and Lydia talk. Robert takes off his sweater. Lydia says "That's a good shirt." Lydia touches Robert's shirt. Robert and Lydia eat falafel. They finish eating falafel. Lydia puts dishes into the dishwasher. Robert gathers crumbs with a wet paper towel. Robert and Lydia walk to Lydia's bedroom. Robert looks at Lydia's back. He thinks "I should make out with her." He thinks "She's really fucked up, though." Robert and Lydia walk outside. They walk to the beach. They walk. Robert looks at the ocean. It's dark. Robert looks at Lydia.

Robert says "Do you want to make out?"

Lydia says "Do you think we should?"

Robert says "No, we shouldn't. I'm sorry. Yeah, I'm sorry I asked that." Robert and Lydia talk. They turn around. They walk. Robert says "Do you want to swim?"

Robert and Lydia talk. They walk to Lydia's parents' house. Robert and Lydia walk into Lydia's parents' house. Lydia turns on the TV. *Maria Full of Grace* is on TV. Robert and Lydia look at the TV.

Lydia says "I really like this movie a lot." Robert and Lydia talk. Lydia turns off the TV. Robert and Lydia walk outside. They get into Robert's car. They drive around the block. They listen to the album *Pop The Glock* by Uffie. They are in front of Lydia's parents' house.

Robert says "Don't you think this is good?" He looks at Lydia.

Lydia says "Yeah what'd you say it's called?" Robert looks at Lydia's parents' house.

Robert says "Uffie." Robert and Lydia talk. Lydia gets out of Robert's car. She walks to her parents' house. She looks at Robert. Robert looks at Lydia. He waves at Lydia. Lydia waves at Robert. She walks into her parents' house. Robert drives. Robert plays the song "Here Comes Success" by Iggy Pop. Robert sees a car pointing diagonally into a tree. There is smoke rising from the car. Robert pulls over. He walks across the street. He takes the key ring out of his pocket. Robert presses a button on the key ring. His car's rear lights turn on. His car's rear lights turn off. Robert puts the key ring into his pocket. Robert takes his cell phone out of his pocket. He looks at the car pointing diagonally into a tree. There are people near the car. Someone near the car says something. Someone else near the car says something. Robert looks at his cell phone. He puts his cell phone into his pocket. Robert walks. He stands in front of the car pointing diagonally into a tree. There is a fat middle-aged woman, a boy with a shaved head, and a girl in a short white dress. Robert says "Is there anyone in the car?"

The fat middle-aged woman says "Yeah, there's still someone inside, but I don't think we can get him out." Robert looks at the car. He looks at the girl in the short white dress. The girl in the short white dress scratches her ass. Her dress moves up a little bit. Robert walks across the street. He takes the key ring out of his pocket. Robert presses a button on the key ring. He opens his car's door. He gets into his car. He closes his car's door. He plays the song "Rebel, Rebel" by David Bowie. He drives to his parents' house. He gets out of his car. He walks into his parents' house. He sits on the couch. He turns on the TV. *The Office* is on TV.

Robert eats a banana. He eats mulberries. Robert smokes a cigarette. He thinks "Sonic Youth has been around for a long time." Robert lies on his bed. He pulls a blanket over his body. Robert turns off his bedside lamp. He hears the building door open. He hears the building door close. Robert stands up. He turns on the overhead light. Robert looks at himself in the mirror. He walks to the living room. Robert sees Jim. Robert and Jim talk. Robert and Jim smoke pot. Jim invites Robert to a Halloween party. Robert and Jim ride bikes to Dan's house. Robert and Jim walk inside. There are people. People wear costumes. People don't wear costumes. Robert drinks beer. Robert sits next to Jill. Jill is dressed as an order of french fries from McDonald's. Robert thinks "I feel caged in, in my life." He thinks "No, my life is okay. I can leave." Robert stands up. He walks to the kitchen. He pours vodka into a glass. He pours orange juice into the glass. Robert walks to the backyard. He drinks vodka and orange juice. Robert is asleep. He is awake. Robert is lying on a small beige couch. He stands up. Robert walks to a small burgundy couch. He lies on the small burgundy couch. Ted is sitting on a reclining chair. Ashley is lying on a large couch. Ted and Ashley are asleep. Robert looks at his cell phone. He walks to the bathroom. Robert lifts the toilet seat. There are cigarette butts in the toilet. Robert leans over the toilet. He punches himself in the stomach. He runs in place. Robert coughs. He washes his hands. He washes his face. Robert walks into the living room. Dan is standing in the living room. Ted and Ashley are awake.

Dan says "Hey Robert. You wanna go to the diner?" Robert looks at Ashley. Robert touches his stomach.

Robert says "Nah, I think I'm gonna go sleep more. Thanks though."

Dan says "Suit yourself." Dan, Ted and Ashley leave. Robert rides his bike. He walks into his building. He walks up stairs. Robert walks into his apartment. He walks into his bedroom. He lies down. He is asleep. Robert is awake. He takes a bath. He reads the story "Community Life" by Lorrie Moore. Robert rides his bike to Whole Foods. He buys arugula, broccoli, pasta sauce, portabello mushrooms and a baguette. Robert rides his bike to his building. He makes dinner. He eats dinner. He makes a video of himself eating dinner. He washes dishes. Robert uploads the video to YouTube.

Robert thinks "Rachel is coming over. I like Rachel. She wears good clothes. I imagine she has a pleasant if distant relationship with her parents." He thinks "We're going to play Scrabble." He thinks "Kissing her would make me feel good. Or better. Something." Robert looks at his cell phone. It's ten p.m. Robert walks outside. He smokes a cigarette. He thinks "I like to smoke cigarettes." Robert walks inside. He walks up stairs. He walks into his apartment. He walks into his bedroom. He checks his email. Robert has a MySpace message from Rachel. It says that Rachel and Ashley are just leaving their house. Robert thinks "Oh." He thinks "She's bringing Ashley." Robert walks to the living room. He sweeps the living room. He walks to the kitchen. He puts water into a tea kettle. He puts the tea kettle on the stove. He turns on the stove. Robert sweeps the kitchen. He opens the refrigerator. He throws out some lettuce. He closes the refrigerator. Robert puts loose tea into a tea ball. He turns off the stove. He puts the tea ball into a teapot. Robert pours hot water into the teapot. Robert puts the teapot on the kitchen table. He picks up three mugs. He puts the mugs on the kitchen table. He moves the mugs around on the kitchen table. Robert touches his forehead. He thinks "Do I have a fever?" Robert looks at his cell phone. He lies on the couch. Robert reads *Anagrams* by Lorrie Moore. Robert's phone rings. Rachel says "We're outside."

Robert says "Okay." Robert walks out of his apartment. He walks down stairs. He opens the door. He says "Hiya." Rachel and Ashley walk inside. Robert walks up stairs. Rachel and Ashley walk up stairs. Rachel and Ashley take off their coats. Robert, Rachel and Ashley talk. They talk about a new restaurant. Robert asks if Rachel and Ashley would like tea. They say that they would. Robert pours tea into the mugs. Robert, Rachel and Ashley play Scrabble. Rachel wins. Robert comes in second. Ashley comes in third. Ashley walks to the bathroom. Robert looks at Rachel. He says "Do you want to play again?"

Rachel says "I think we're gonna go home. I have work tomorrow at nine and it's already, what?" Rachel looks at her cell phone. "Yeah, it's quarter to twelve. But we should definitely do something soon." Ashley walks into the living room. Rachel says "Robert, do you mind walking us halfway home?"

Robert says "Of course, yeah. Sure." Robert, Rachel and Ashley walk. It's cold. They talk. They smoke cigarettes. They say goodbye. Robert walks home. He plays the song "I Shall Be Released" by The Band three times. He turns off his laptop computer. Robert puts a blanket on his bedroom floor. He turns off the lights. Robert lies on the blanket on the floor. He stands up. He lies on his bed. He stands up. Robert takes a shower. He looks at himself in the mirror. Robert lies on his bed.

Robert looks out the window. He stands up. He sits near his laptop computer. He looks at pornography. Robert thinks

"When I look at pornography I mostly focus on facial cum-shots. I should focus on something else, I think. I don't know." Robert looks at himself in the mirror. He plays the song "Underneath It All" by No Doubt. Robert ejaculates. He walks to the bathroom. He takes a shower. He washes his penis. He thinks "My penis feels bad." Robert walks into his bedroom. He looks at himself in the mirror. He looks out the window. He puts on underwear. He thinks "My penis." Robert puts on jeans. He puts on a thermal undershirt. Robert puts on a pink t-shirt with a drawing of a rabbit and the words "The Ballet." Robert lies on his bed. Robert's cat lies on Robert's stomach. Robert looks at the ceiling. He closes his eyes. He takes a deep breath. Robert's cat jumps off of Robert's stomach. Robert's cat leaves. Robert thinks "Okay."

Robert plays the song "I'm Insane" by Sonic Youth. He nods his head. Robert looks at his cat. He puts on shoes. He puts on a light sweater. He looks at his apartment. He walks out of his apartment. He walks down stairs. He walks outside. He walks to a thrift store. He looks at a children's book about time. He looks at a vintage Lacoste tennis shirt. He touches the shirt. Robert walks outside. He walks to his building. He sits on his stoop. He smokes a cigarette. He walks into his building. He walks up stairs. He walks into his apartment. Robert walks into his bedroom. He looks out the window. Robert closes the curtains. He lies on his bed.

Robert is awake. There is a bottle of Budweiser beer on Robert's nightstand. Robert looks at the bottle of Budweiser beer. The bottle of Budweiser beer is half empty. Robert touches the bottle. The bottle is cool. Robert thinks "Good." Robert looks at his cat. He looks at two collared shirts and a pair of underwear on the floor. He looks at his hamper. He thinks "Hamper." He thinks "I should do laundry." Robert looks at his alarm clock. He looks at the curtains. Robert stands up. He buttons his jeans. Robert plays the song "Diamonds and Pearls" by Prince. He looks at himself in the mirror. He thinks "I don't know what to do. About my complexion. It seems shitty."

Robert is drinking a bottle of Yuengling lager. He is watching *The Office*. He laughs. He finishes drinking the bottle of Yuengling lager. A commercial comes on. Robert stands up. He walks to the refrigerator. He opens the refrigerator. He looks at a six-pack of bottles of Yuengling lager. There are five bottles of Yuengling lager left. Robert picks up a bottle of Yuengling lager. Robert closes the refrigerator. He looks at the bottle of Yuengling lager. He opens it. Robert walks to the couch. He sits on the couch. He drinks Yuengling lager. He watches *The Office*. He drinks Yuengling lager. Robert looks at his cat. Robert turns off the TV. Robert turns on a lamp. He picks up the book *What We Talk About When We Talk About Love* by Raymond Carver. He reads the story "Compartments." He drinks Yuengling lager. He reads the story "A Small, Good Thing." He thinks "It's kind of easy to be comfortable in America." He looks at his cell phone. It's ten p.m. Robert walks to the refrigerator. He opens the refrigerator. Robert picks up a bottle of Yuengling lager. He closes the refrigerator. He walks to his bedroom. He sits near his laptop computer. He looks at the Wikipedia entry for Philip K. Dick. He looks at his bank statement. He looks at a take-out menu for a Japanese restaurant. Robert thinks "When I walked to the library earlier I wasn't sure what was happening. The people and houses..." He looks at his cat. Robert opens iTunes. He makes a playlist. He makes the first song "Because The Night" by Patti Smith. He makes the second song "Red & Blue Jeans" by The Promise Ring. Robert makes the third song "Glory Days" by Bruce Springsteen. He makes the fourth song "(Strawberry Ann) Switzerland" by Braid.

Robert is standing in the shower. He turns off the shower. Robert walks into his bedroom. He looks at himself in the mirror. He touches his penis. He is looking at himself in the mirror. Robert thinks "I should shave." He looks at his laptop computer. He looks at pornography on his laptop computer. He masturbates. Robert walks to the bathroom. He walks into the shower. He turns on the shower. Water comes from the showerhead. Robert washes his penis. He washes his hands. He turns off the shower. He walks into his bedroom. He turns off the overhead light. He lies on his bed. He is naked. Robert looks out the window. He thinks "Everything is so stupid. So funny." Robert pulls a blanket over his body. Robert covers his face with his left hand. He moves his left hand back on his head. His left hand is in his hair.

Robert says "I don't have what you want." He looks at his cat. He says "I don't have the capacity to love." Robert rubs his foot against his cat's back. Robert peels the skin off of garlic cloves. He puts the skinned garlic cloves into his food processor. He turns on his food processor. He walks to the refrigerator. He opens the refrigerator. Robert picks up a container of tahini. He closes the refrigerator. Robert makes hummus. He puts hummus and mustard greens on an everything bagel. He plays the album *Slanted & Enchanted* by Pavement. He sits at the kitchen table. He eats the everything bagel with hummus and mustard greens. Robert walks to his bedroom. Robert's cat is lying on Robert's bed. Robert looks at his cat. He touches his cat. Robert thinks "I want to smoke pot. No, I guess I don't."

Robert thinks "If I get Chinese food I'll feel okay for as long as it takes to eat the Chinese food. If I get twice as much Chinese food I'll feel okay for twice as long."

Robert looks out the window. It's Friday night. Robert thinks "Really heavy blankets, so when you get under them you can't move. I think I've been in a bed with blankets like that one time, or else I was just really tired. That was when I did painkillers." He thinks "Painkillers." Robert checks his email. He looks at his shoes. He thinks "What should I have done differently?" He thinks "I have a sore throat." Robert searches "vintage ralph lauren" on eBay. He looks at his bank statement. Robert listens to the song "Gold Soundz" by Pavement. He listens to the song "Gold Soundz" by Pavement. He listens to the song "Gold Soundz" by Pavement. He looks at pictures of Lil Wayne on the internet.

Robert looks at the sky. The sky is gray. Robert rides his bike. He stands in front of Jill's building. He calls Jill. The door opens. Jill walks outside. Jill says "Hi."

Robert says "Hi." He puts his cell phone into his pocket.

Jill says "Hi." She says "Come in." Jill walks into her building. Robert walks into Jill's building. They walk up stairs. They walk into Jill's apartment. Robert leans his bike against a radiator. He says "Where should I put this?"

Jill says "There is fine." Robert and Jill walk to Jill's kitchen. There is a plate of steamed broccoli and hot sauce on the kitchen table. Jill says "Do you want something to eat?"

Robert says "What do you have?"

Jill says "I don't know. Look." Robert opens the refrigerator. The light in the refrigerator doesn't come on. Robert looks at a glass pitcher. He picks up the glass pitcher.

Robert says "What's this?"

Jill says "Homemade cider. Do you want some?"

Robert says "Oh. Sure."

Jill says "Really?"

Robert says "Yeah I guess." Jill stands up. She pours cider into a glass.

Jill says "That's probably a lot." Robert sits down. Robert and Jill talk. Robert takes an avocado out of his book bag. He takes a bagel out of his book bag. Robert cuts the bagel in half. He spreads the avocado on the bagel. He eats the bagel. Robert drinks cider. Robert and Jill walk to Jill's living room. They sit on the couch. They watch *The City of Lost Children.*

Robert says "Are the subtitles on?"

Jill says "Yeah." They watch *The City of Lost Children.* Jill says "Oh I guess they aren't." Jill turns the subtitles on. Robert and Jill watch *The City of Lost Children. The City of Lost Children* starts to skip a lot. Robert thinks "I don't like Jill." Robert and Jill walk to a diner. Robert and Jill sit in a booth. Jill's roommate is a waitress. She walks to Robert and Jill's booth. Robert, Jill and Jill's roommate talk. Jill asks her roommate if she can have a milkshake for free.

Robert looks at a container of cat medicine. He unscrews the plastic dropper from the container of cat medicine. Robert smells the cat medicine. He inserts the plastic dropper into the container of cat medicine. He squeezes the dropper. Cat medicine fills the dropper. Robert walks to his cat. He holds his cat's mouth open. He inserts the plastic dropper into his cat's mouth. He squeezes the plastic dropper. He looks at his cat. Robert takes the dropper out of his cat's mouth. He screws the plastic dropper into the container of cat medicine. He puts the container of cat medicine in a drawer. Robert walks to his bedroom. He plays the album *The Slow Wonder* by A.C. Newman. He calls Jill. He doesn't leave a voicemail. Robert thinks "Um." Robert plays the album *No Gods, No Managers* by Choking Victim. He gets a text message from Jill. Jill's text message says "I'm at a party." Robert takes a shower. He takes four sweaters out of his closet. He puts them on his bed. Robert gets a text message from Jill. It says "How are you?"

Robert is lying on his stomach. He thinks "My bedroom is clean." Robert walks to his laptop computer. He checks his email. Robert plays the song "Lord Anthony" by Belle & Sebastian. He sits in a chair. He thinks "I want to like the way someone looks and to like other things about them a lot and have it be mutual and not have anything bad happen right away." Robert walks to the living room. He looks at his cat. Robert walks outside. He looks at the sky. The sky is gray. Robert walks to the laundromat. He thinks "I'll buy a lot of carrots and just drink a lot of carrot juice tonight." He takes clothing out of a washing machine. He puts clothing into a dryer. Robert puts quarters into the dryer.

Robert's cat makes a sound. Robert eats a salad. Robert gets vinegar on his t-shirt. He looks at the book *Shopgirl* by Steve Martin. Robert thinks "*Get small.*" He pours water into a glass. He walks outside. He drinks water. Robert is walking. He walks to a park. There are leaves on the ground. The leaves are brown and yellow. Robert thinks "I know what sound I would hear if I stepped on leaves."

Robert is reading the book *Chilly Scenes of Winter* by Ann Beattie. Robert smokes a cigarette. Robert looks out the window. He walks to the bathroom. He looks at himself in the mirror. He ashes his cigarette into the sink. Robert washes his hands. He looks at himself in the mirror. Robert walks into his bedroom. He looks at his cell phone. Robert thinks "I know that nothing matters but I still live as though I think that something matters. No, maybe I don't. That's what I should do, though. No, I don't know."

Robert looks at Jill. Jill is asleep. It's dark. Robert and Jill are lying in Robert's bed. Robert looks out the window. He thinks "I wish Jill wasn't sleeping in my bed." He thinks "I'm warm. I'm comfortable." Robert stands up. He walks to his laptop computer. Robert checks his email. He looks at Jill. Robert thinks "Jill is okay-looking." Robert walks to the bathroom. He looks at himself in the mirror. He walks into his bedroom. He looks at Jill. Robert lies on his bed. He is asleep. He is awake. He looks at Jill. He thinks "I shouldn't let girls I don't really like or something sleep in my bed." He thinks "I shouldn't call girls I don't really like or something. Shouldn't answer my phone when girls I don't really like or something call me." Robert stands up. He walks to the kitchen. He washes dishes. He walks to his bedroom. He looks at Jill. He checks his email.

Robert takes his keys out of his pocket. There is a bottle opener on Robert's key ring. The bottle opener shows a detail from the cover art for the album *Earthquake Glue* by Guided By Voices. Robert touches the bottle opener. He puts his keys into his pocket. Robert thinks "What should I do? I feel really tired." Robert picks up a lid. He looks at water. The water isn't boiling. Robert puts the lid on a pot. Robert walks to the couch. Robert sits on the couch. He looks at his cat. He says "Fuck you, fucker." He touches his cat. Robert reads the story "Vermont" by Ann Beattie. Robert walks to the kitchen. He takes the lid off the pot. He looks at the water. He thinks "Ann Beattie." Robert looks at the water. He thinks "Vermont." The water is boiling. Robert puts spaghetti into the water. Robert walks to the couch. He sits on the couch. Robert touches his cat. He says "You douchebag." He pets his cat. He smacks his cat's ass. Robert's cat leaves. Robert lies on the couch. He unbuttons his jeans. He puts his hand inside his underwear. He holds his penis. He closes his eyes. Robert opens his eyes. He takes his hand out of his underwear. He buttons his jeans. Robert stands up. He walks into the kitchen. He washes his hands. Robert looks at spaghetti. He pours spaghetti into a colander. Robert looks at spaghetti. Robert puts spaghetti on a plate. He puts pasta sauce on the spaghetti. He carries the plate to the kitchen table. Robert eats spaghetti. He looks at the plate. Robert takes his cell phone out of his pocket. He puts his cell phone into his pocket. Robert walks to his bedroom. He looks at his bed. He thinks "Okay." Robert inhales. He exhales. He lies on his bed. Robert plays the album *You Forgot It In People* by Broken Social Scene. The song "Anthems for a Seventeen Year-Old Girl" is playing. Robert sings along to "Anthems for a Seventeen Year-Old Girl." He stands up. He walks to his laptop computer. Robert looks at Facebook. Jill wrote on Robert's wall. She wrote "I had fun." Robert thinks *"The Best of Jill Hives."* Robert hears the building door open. He hears the building door close. Robert hears foot-steps. Robert hears a knock on his bedroom door. Robert says "Come in." Jim walks into Robert's bedroom. Robert and Jim talk. Robert says "Jim, do you know where I could buy a big box of matches?" Robert and Jim talk. Jim leaves.

It's Thanksgiving. Robert is walking. He is next to train tracks. He is smoking a cigarette. He sees people. He is walking towards the people. He is near the people. The people are boys. One of the boys says "Hey, you have an extra cigarette?" Robert looks at the boy.

Robert says "Sor– uh, yeah." The boy walks to Robert. Robert hands the boy a cigarette.

The boy says "Thanks." The boy turns. The boy walks to the boys.

Robert says "Do you need a light?"

The boy says "Oh. Yeah." The boy turns. He looks at Robert. He walks to Robert. Robert strikes a match. He holds it to the boy's cigarette. The cigarette doesn't light.

Robert says "Shit. Sorry."

One of the boys says "I have a lighter." The boy turns. He walks to the boys.

Robert says "See ya." Robert walks. He drops his cigarette. Robert is near a bridge. There is a man and a woman. The man and the woman are holding fishing rods. Robert says "Any luck?"

The woman says "Some babies. Had to throw 'em back."

The man says "Got one nice one, though." The man lifts his hands in the air. He holds them a distance apart from one another. The man smiles. Robert smiles.

Robert says "Well, good luck."

The woman says "Thanks, baby." The woman looks at Robert. Robert walks.

Robert sends Jill a text message. It says "Hi." Robert plays the album *We Have the Facts and We're Voting Yes* by Death Cab for Cutie. Robert smokes a cigarette. He thinks "This cigarette tastes bad." He looks at the cigarette. He smokes the cigarette. The song "Company Calls" is playing. Robert thinks "This song is a good song." Robert looks out the window. He stands up. He walks into the bathroom. He looks at the toilet. He looks at the shower. He looks at the book *Cosmopolis* by Don DeLillo. Robert pees. He washes his hands. He walks into his bedroom. He looks at his cell phone.

It's raining. Robert is riding his bike. He is in front of his building. Robert walks into his building. He walks up stairs. He walks into his apartment. It's dark. Robert thinks "Jim isn't here." Robert walks into the kitchen. He pours water into a glass. He drinks the water. He pours water into the glass. Robert knocks on Jim's bedroom door. Robert opens Jim's bedroom door. It's dark. It smells like sweat. Robert closes Jim's bedroom door. Robert walks into his bedroom.

He turns on the overhead light. He looks at his bed. Robert lies on his bed. He looks at the ceiling. Robert looks at his cell phone. Robert opens the window. He rubs his forefinger against the screen in the window.

Robert walks into his building. He walks up stairs. He walks into his apartment. It's cold. Robert looks at his cat. Robert laughs. He walks into his bedroom. He checks his email. Four people wrote on Robert's Facebook wall. Robert calls Jill. Jill says "Happy birthday."

Robert says "Thanks Jill."

Jill says "How are you?'

Robert says "I'm okay. I'm okay."

Jill says "What did you do for your birthday?"

Robert says "Nothing really. I mean, I went to work and then I went out to dinner with my friends."

Jill says "Oh, who'd you go out with?"

Robert says "Karen and Jason."

Jill says "Who?" Robert thinks "Why did I call Jill?"

Robert says "People I work with."

Jill says "Oh cool."

Robert says "It's pretty late, huh?"

Jill says "Yeah."

Robert says "I'm—"

Jill says "Are you gay?"

Robert says "No." He says "But I was kind of thinking about saying that."

Jill says "Why?"

Robert says "I thought it would be easier, or something." Robert coughs.

Jill says "No. No, I think I know what you're saying. That's totally cool though." She says "I would still want to hang out with you though, just as whatever or something."

Robert says "Yeah." He says "Yeah totally."

Jill says "Do you want to see a movie? Like, as friends? We can bring forties."

Robert says "Sure." He says "Yeah, what movie do you want to see?"

Jill says "I don't really know what's playing. You said something about a new *Blade Runner* director's cut or something the other day?"

Robert says "Oh yeah." He looks at his cat. Robert says "Yeah, I don't really think I want to see that anymore."

Jill says "That's fine. I kind of wanted to see *Juno*."

Robert says "Yeah? I would see that. We should see that."

Jill says "I'm off tomorrow. Do you have work?"

Robert says "Yeah, but I get out at six. I'll call you before that, okay?"

Jill says "Yeah, that's great. Goodnight Robert. Happy birthday."

Robert says "Happy birthday, Jill. Goodnight." Robert smokes a cigarette. He walks into the kitchen. Robert pours water into a glass. He looks at the glass. He puts the glass on the counter. Robert walks into his bedroom. He lies on his bed. He looks at his cat. He plays the album *Electric Version* by The New Pornographers.

Robert is driving. Lydia is sitting next to Robert. Robert parks his car. Robert and Lydia get out of Robert's car. They walk towards a house. Casey's car pulls up. Casey parks his car. Casey gets out of his car. Two young men get out of Casey's car. Robert and Lydia greet Casey and the young men. Everyone walks into the house. Mark and Ian are inside the house. Two young women are inside the house. Everyone greets one another. Everyone sits down. Mark is drinking water out of a Pyrex measuring cup. Mark is holding a matchbox. Mark opens the matchbox. There are three small pills inside the matchbox. Robert walks towards the door. Mark says "Where are you going?"

Robert says "I'm gonna go smoke a cigarette."

Mark says "I'm gonna go smoke a cigarette with Robert." Robert and Mark walk outside. They smoke cigarettes. Robert and Mark talk.

Robert says "What are you doing, man?"

Mark says "I'm just tryin' to live man." Lydia walks outside. Her hair is dyed black. Lydia walks inside. Robert thinks "She looks good, sort of." Casey and Ian walk outside. Robert, Mark, Casey and Ian smoke pot. They walk inside. Robert walks into the bathroom. He pees. He thinks "Ian doesn't like me." He walks out of the bathroom. Robert, Mark and Lydia are sitting together. Casey and Ian are sitting together. Robert thinks "Ian looks distressed. He's wearing distressed jeans from American Eagle." He thinks "I've never had a conversation with Ian in my life." Mark opens the matchbox.

Lydia says "Can I buy a Xanax, Mark?"

Robert says "Don't sell her any pills." He thinks "I thought I would say that quieter." Mark doesn't sell Lydia any pills. Robert thinks "That's good, but he just didn't sell her any pills because he wants to take them all himself."

Lydia says "Do you want to go soon?"

Robert says "Yeah." Robert and Lydia say goodbye to everyone. They walk outside. They get into Robert's car. Robert thinks "I'm high." Robert is driving. There is a 7-Eleven. Robert double parks in front of the 7-Eleven. Robert thinks "If I was a cop and I saw a car double parked at three a.m. at a 7-Eleven I would investigate or something. No, I don't know what cops do." Robert and Lydia walk into the 7-Eleven. Robert looks at Lydia. He says "Hurry." Lydia looks at Robert. She buys Vitaminwater. They walk outside. It's cold. They get into Robert's car. Robert is driving.

Lydia says "I think it was fucked of you to tell Mark not to sell me pills."

Robert is lying on his bed. He is sweating. Robert looks at a fan. Robert looks out the window. He looks at a fenced-in area across the street. Robert thinks "I want to like being around someone a lot. I want to go to a bar with someone I like. I want to sit at a table and feel good about the person sitting across from me. Sitting next to me." Robert looks at his cat. He looks out the window. Robert looks at his alarm clock. He thinks "I have work in two hours." Robert turns on the radio. He turns off the radio. He walks to the bathroom. He pees. Robert looks at the litter box. He thinks "I'm glad I live in America, I think." Robert takes a shower. Robert walks into his bedroom. He sits on his bed. He puts on socks. He puts on underwear. He puts on jeans. He puts on a t-shirt. He takes off the t-shirt. He puts on a collared shirt. Robert looks at a glass of water. He drinks from the glass of water. The album *Strawberry Jam* by Animal Collective is playing. Robert checks his email. Robert has no new email. Robert looks at his cat. He thinks "Animal Collective are probably happy." Robert laughs. He thinks "I scare myself when I laugh." Robert pulls down his jeans. He pulls down his underwear. He looks at his penis. He jerks his penis. Robert's penis is flaccid. Robert pulls up his underwear. He pulls up his jeans. He rubs his sleeve against his eyes. He looks at himself in the mirror. Robert undoes the top button on his shirt. He thinks "I have to go to work. I wish work was over."

Robert calls Alison. He doesn't leave a message. He takes a shower. The album *Moon Pix* by Cat Power is playing. Robert's phone rings. Robert looks at his phone. He turns down the volume. Robert answers his phone. He says "Alison."

Alison says "Hi." Robert turns off the light. He lies on his bed.

Robert says "How are you?"

Alison says "I'm okay." She says "How are you?"

Robert says "I don't know. Dumb. My life is dumb."

Alison says "Yeah?"

Robert says "I don't know." He says "We haven't spoken in a while."

Alison says "Yeah."

Robert says "I made you mad or something the last time we spoke."

Alison says "Yeah."

Robert says "I'm sorry."

Alison says "It's okay." Robert and Alison talk. There are several periods of silence spanning between five and fifteen seconds.

Robert says "I just kind of don't really have any other close friends."

Alison says "Have you given any thought to why that might be?" She says "You call me whenever you feel bad and want to feel better. I'm the one you call every time. But when I feel bad and I call you, it's like you don't even try. You just act like it's a joke, whatever's happening in my life." She says "So I don't call you when I feel bad anymore, and I don't pick up all the time when you call. It's not my responsibility. I don't have to make you feel better." Robert and Alison talk.

Robert says "Well, goodbye." It's cold. Robert looks at his bookshelf. He closes the window. Robert stands up. He turns on the overhead light. He opens his closet door. He looks at a blanket. Robert puts the blanket on the floor. He lies on the blanket on the floor. Robert stands up. He picks up the blanket. He puts the blanket on his bed. Robert turns off the overhead light. He lies on his bed. He rubs a pillowcase against his nose. He thinks, "I want to watch

Frasier with my dad." Robert looks at his cell phone. He looks at his cat.

Robert's alarm clock goes off. He thinks "I hope I didn't say anything stupid last night." He coughs. Robert turns off his alarm clock. He stands up. He looks at himself in the mirror. He walks into the bathroom. He takes a shower. He thinks "My face is okay."

Robert walks to a vintage clothing store. He walks inside. He thinks "They're going to close soon. I'm nervous." Robert looks at vintage clothing. He touches vintage clothing. He touches a vintage cardigan. He puts on the cardigan. He thinks "This fits well." He looks at himself in the mirror. Robert takes off the cardigan. He looks at the price tag. He looks at two small holes. One small hole is on the left shoulder. One small hole is on the right elbow. Robert thinks "What should I do?" He looks at a couple. He thinks "They should tell me it looks good. They should tell me to buy it." He looks at the couple. He puts the cardigan on a hanger. He puts the hanger on a rack. Robert looks at the ceiling. He looks at the floor. Robert thinks "What article of vintage clothing is going to make me feel happy?"

Robert is lying on his bed. A candle is burning. It's dark. Robert's bedroom door is closed. Robert thinks "Something should happen." Robert is lying on his bed. Robert's cell phone rings. Robert says "Hello."

Tom says "Hey." Robert and Tom talk. They stop talking. Robert stands up. He walks into the kitchen. He puts cat food into a bowl. He puts water into a bowl. He walks into his bedroom. He looks at himself in the mirror. He puts on a hat. He makes a face.

Robert, Tom, Ryan and Nancy get out of Ryan's car. They pick up bags. They walk to Tom's dad's house. They walk into Tom's dad's house. They put down their bags. They drink beer. Robert takes pictures with his digital camera. He puts his digital camera on a coffee table. Tom takes pictures with Robert's digital camera. Robert walks outside. There is a stream. Robert smokes a cigarette. He takes his cell phone out of his jacket pocket. He looks at his cell phone. Robert thinks "It's so nice here." He thinks "I want to call someone." He put his cell phone into his jacket pocket. He looks at the stream. Ryan comes outside. He stands near Robert. He looks at Robert. Ryan says "It's so nice here."

Robert says "Yeah." Ryan takes a pack of cigarettes out of his pants pocket. Ryan takes a cigarette from the pack. Ryan puts the pack back into his pants pocket. Ryan puts the cigarette in his mouth. He takes the cigarette out of his mouth.

Ryan says "Hey, do you have a lighter?"

Robert says "Oh, yeah." Robert takes a lighter out of his pocket. He hands Ryan the lighter. Ryan puts the cigarette back in his mouth.

Ryan says "Thanks." Ryan lights the cigarette. He hands Robert the lighter. Ryan looks at the stream. Robert puts the lighter in his pocket. Robert looks at the stream.

Robert says "That was a long drive."

Ryan says "Yeah."

Robert says "You and Nancy did a really good job. When I drove up last time it took a lot longer."

Robert's alarm clock goes off. Robert turns off his alarm clock. Robert stands up. He plays the song "Fireman" by Lil Wayne. He checks his email. Robert thinks "*Fireman, fa fa fa fireman.*" Robert walks into the kitchen. He makes carrot juice. He drinks carrot juice. He cleans the juicer. Robert walks to the couch. He lies on the couch. Robert walks into the bathroom. He takes a shower. He walks into his bedroom. He looks at his cat. Robert makes his bed. He sweeps his bedroom floor. Robert looks out the window. He sits on his bed. He stands up.

Robert looks at Gmail. Sam is on Gmail. Robert says "Hi." Sam says "Hi." Robert thinks "I don't have anything to say to Sam." Robert looks at his bedroom. He thinks "What am I doing?" He thinks "I want to smoke a cigarette." He thinks "No." He thinks "I feel sick." Robert thinks "My lease is going to end some day." Mitchel is on Gmail.

Mitchel says "Hey." Robert takes off his shoes. He thinks "What do people in my situation do?" He walks to his bed. He lies on his bed.

Tom says "You should chew your food more." Robert chews falafel. He swallows falafel.

Robert says "Yeah. Yeah I don't chew enough. People that are into macrobiotics are all about chewing. I would suck at macrobiotics."

Tom says "Yeah you would."

A waitress walks to Robert and Tom's table. She says "How is everything?"

Tom says "It's great." Robert chews. The waitress leaves. Tom drinks mint iced tea. Robert drinks mint iced tea. Tom says "I love mint iced tea." Robert thinks "I should do sit-ups. Every day. Fifty sit-ups. When I wake up. And before bed." Tom drinks mint iced tea. Robert looks at the waitress. The waitress is wearing a skirt. Robert looks at Tom.

Robert says "I've been really tired lately."

Robert is asleep. He's awake. It's noon. Robert thinks "My throat hurts." He thinks "I felt happy before I went to sleep last night. I know why I felt happy. I know I should feel happy." Robert stands up. He puts clothing into a laundry bag. He puts a bottle of laundry detergent into the laundry bag. Robert walks to the living room. Jim is lying on the couch. Jim is playing *Castlevania* on Nintendo. Jim asks Robert if he's doing laundry. Robert says yes. Jim says "Do you think there'll be room in the machine for my sheets? Jackie and Dave had sex on 'em when they stayed here, so I've just been sleeping on the couch the past couple nights."

Robert says "Yeah alright." Robert walks into Jim's bedroom. He puts Jim's sheets into the laundry bag. Robert walks into the living room. Robert and Jim talk. Robert walks outside. It's cold. Robert walks to the laundromat. He puts clothing and sheets into a washing machine. He puts laundry detergent into the washing machine. He puts quarters into the washing machine. Robert walks to the bank. He fills out a deposit slip. He signs a check. Robert walks to a bank teller. He hands the deposit slip and the check to the bank teller. The bank teller is talking to another bank teller.

The other bank teller says "Yeah, my buddy's a valet, some steak place in midtown. The other day Jay-Z came in, gave him a hundred-dollar tip."

Robert's bank teller says "Hell, if I was Jay-Z I might just give out hundred-dollar tips myself." Robert's bank teller says something.

Robert says "What?" Robert's bank teller is typing.

Robert's bank teller says "If you were rich like that, wouldn't you do something like that?"

Robert says "Oh. Yeah." Robert's bank teller hands Robert a receipt.

Robert's bank teller says "Have a great day."

Robert says "Thank you." Robert walks outside. He thinks "I wish I was Jay-Z. I wish I was rich like that." He walks to the laundromat. He takes clothing and sheets out of the washing machine. He puts clothing and sheets into a dryer. He puts quarters into the dryer.

Robert is reading *Taking Care* by Joy Williams. Robert's cell phone rings. Robert picks up his cell phone. He says "Hi." Jim asks if he can borrow Robert's bike. Robert says yes. Robert reads *Taking Care* by Joy Williams. He stands up. He checks his email. He lies on his bed. He reads *Taking Care* by Joy Williams. Robert hears the apartment door open. He hears the apartment door close. Robert hears a knock on his bedroom door. Robert says "Come in." Jim walks into Robert's bedroom. Robert and Jim talk.

Jim says "I'm going over to Ashley and Rachel's, you wanna come?"

Robert says "There's only one bike."

Jim says "I don't mind walking if it's with someone."

Robert says "Oh. Then yeah I'll come. Give me a minute." Jim leaves. Jim closes Robert's bedroom door. Robert takes his clothes off. He thinks "What should I wear? I like Rachel." He thinks "I guess I'm not going to do anything with Rachel, I guess it doesn't matter." He thinks "What should I wear?"

Jim says "We should kind of hurry so we can make it to the beer store before it closes."

Robert says "Oh yeah." Robert puts on clothes. He turns off the overhead light. He walks to the living room. Robert and Jim walk outside. They walk to a beer store. It's closed. They walk to a beer store. It's closed. They walk to a beer store. It's closed. Robert and Jim walk to Rachel and Ashley's building. Jim takes a key ring out of his pocket. Jim unlocks the door.

Jim says "I like that I have keys to Ashley and Rachel's apartment." Robert and Jim walk into Rachel and Ashley's building. They walk into Rachel and Ashley's apartment. Jim says "I like that Ashley and Rachel's apartment has a basement." Robert and Jim walk into the basement. Rachel, Ashley, Eric and Cody are there. People greet one another. Jim says "We went to three beer stores and all three were closed. They close at one now. It's some bullshit."

Robert says "It's fucking bullshit."

Eric says "That would have been awesome if you had gotten beer." He says "Because then we would have beer." Rachel and Cody are sitting on a couch. Cody is rolling a joint. Ashley and Rachel look drunk. Robert thinks "I should say something so people know I don't hate them or something. Doesn't everyone always think I hate them? Because I never say anything?" Eric touches an iPod. Robert looks at Rachel. Rachel's head is on Cody's shoulder. Her eyes are closed. Eric plays the album *Isn't Anything* by My Bloody Valentine. Robert looks at the iPod.

Robert says "I've never heard this band before."

Eric says "Yeah me neither. I've heard *of* them."

Robert says "Me too." Cody finishes rolling the joint. Cody lights the joint. He passes the joint. People smoke the joint. Robert smokes the joint. He coughs. Robert passes the joint. Eric looks at Robert. Robert looks at Eric. He looks at Ashley. Ashley is holding the joint. She smokes the joint.

Ashley says "It's done." Rachel walks up stairs. Cody walks up stairs. There is a pack of cigarettes on the coffee table. Eric picks up the pack of cigarettes. He opens the pack of cigarettes.

Eric says "Ooh." He takes a cigarette from the pack of cigarettes. Eric puts the cigarette behind his ear.

Jim says "Do you guys wanna hit the road?"

Eric says "Yeah." He says "Yeah just a second." Eric is rolling a joint.

Ashley says "That's Cody's weed." Eric looks at Ashley.

Eric says "I'm a bad man." Eric is wearing a leather jacket. Eric says "I wear a leather jacket and I am a bad man. I put on this leather jacket, and I am a bad man. I only have one job: to be bad." Eric finishes rolling the joint. He says "I was going to smoke this on the way home, but do you want to smoke some more, Ashley?"

Ashley says "No. Thanks Eric." Robert, Jim, Eric and Ashley talk. They walk up stairs.

Eric says "Goodnight Ashley. Goodnight other friends." Robert, Jim and Eric walk out of Rachel and Ashley's apartment. They walk out of Rachel and Ashley's building. Robert, Jim and Eric smoke the joint. They walk to Eric's building. They walk into Eric's building. They walk up stairs. They walk into Eric's apartment. They walk into Eric's bedroom. Robert sees his scarf. He picks it up. There is a cigarette burn on Robert's scarf. Robert puts on his scarf. He thinks "I'm glad I found my scarf. This night was good now." Robert, Jim and Eric look at something on Eric's computer. Robert's cell phone rings. Robert looks at his cell phone. He walks into the hallway. He walks into the bathroom. He sits on the toilet. He answers his cell phone. Robert and Tom talk. Robert tells Tom about seeing Rachel put her head on Cody's shoulder. He thinks "Can Jim and Eric hear me? Do they care? Do I?" Robert and Tom stop talking. Robert walks into Eric's bedroom. Robert, Jim

and Eric look at something on Eric's computer. Everyone
says goodbye. Robert and Jim walk outside. They walk to
their building. They walk into their building. They walk
up stairs. They walk into their apartment. Robert makes a
sandwich. He makes a sandwich. Robert walks to the couch.
He hands Jim a sandwich.

Jim says "Thanks." Robert and Jim watch the movie
Polyester. They each eat a sandwich. Robert thinks "This
movie has really good production values."

Robert says "I'm going to bed."

Jim says "Me too."

Robert says "Goodnight Jim."

Jim says "'Night."

Robert reads the story "Charity" by Joy Williams. He looks
out the window. A boy is knocking on a door. A girl is
standing next to him. Another boy is standing near the corner. The second boy says "Nah, it's between Sixth and Sev-
enth." Robert closes the window. He looks at a candlestick.
He thinks "When it's nighttime I can light candles. I should
put on a sweater. I should make carrot juice." Robert puts
on a sweater. He thinks "I should constantly be thinking of
what I can do to improve myself." Robert laughs. He thinks
"I'm clean." Robert walks to the kitchen. He makes carrot
juice. He drinks carrot juice. He cleans the juicer. He looks
at the refrigerator. There isn't any food in the refrigerator.
He thinks "There was a lot of good food in the refrigerator
at one point. I ate a lot of good food."

Robert's alarm clock goes off. Robert is awake. Robert thinks "I don't have work today." He turns off his alarm clock. Robert is asleep. He is awake. Robert plays the song "Friend of the Devil" by the Grateful Dead. He stands up. Robert looks at his alarm clock. It's 11:45 a.m. Robert picks up his Game Boy. He plays Tetris. He puts down his Game Boy. Robert stands up. He opens his bedroom door. Robert's cat walks into Robert's bedroom. Robert walks into the bathroom. Robert brushes his teeth. He walks into the living room. He puts on a jacket. He walks out of his apartment. He walks down stairs. He walks out of his building. He walks to Pathmark. He walks into Pathmark. Robert buys a lemon and two bags of cat food. He walks outside. It's cold. Robert walks to his building. He walks into his building. He walks up stairs.

Robert is at a bar. The song "Shady Lane" by Pavement is playing. Robert is singing along to "Shady Lane." Ted is smoking a clove cigarette. Laura says "Who is this?"

Robert says "Pavement."

Laura says "I don't really know Caveman." Robert thinks "I want a clove cigarette."

Robert says "What?"

Laura says "I've never really heard too much Caveman."

Robert says "No. Pavement."

Laura says "What?"

Robert says "This is that band, Pavement."

Laura says "Oh. Oh... Pavement. Yeah, I never really got into them. I'm a huge Stephen Malkmus fan, though. 'No

More Shoes' has got to be like one of my all-time faves."
Robert says "Yeah." Robert says "Ted, can I get a cigarette?"
Ted says "Sure." Ted picks up his glass of beer. He
moves it towards Robert. Robert looks at Ted. Ted smiles.
Ted moves his glass of beer back to its original position. He
takes a pack of clove cigarettes out of his jacket pocket. He
hands Robert a clove cigarette. He hands Robert a lighter.
Robert says "Thank you." He thinks "Ted is pretty
drunk." Robert, Ted and Laura talk. The song "Fight Test"
by The Flaming Lips is playing. The song "Float On" by
Modest Mouse is playing.

Robert is carrying two bananas and a can of black beans.
It's dark. It's cold. Robert is wearing a hat. He is wearing
a hoodie. Robert's hood covers his hat. Robert thinks "It's
probably okay working the late shift at Pathmark. It's probably funny. You just try to stay awake. And then later you
can go to sleep." Robert walks into his building. He walks
up stairs. He walks into his apartment. Robert walks into
his bedroom. Robert eats a banana. He lies on his bed. He
reads the label on the can of black beans. Robert is asleep.
He is awake. Robert looks at his alarm clock. It's five fifty
a.m. Robert looks out the window. It's raining.

Robert walks to an organic market. He walks into the organic market. A tattooed woman is standing behind the cash
register. Robert looks at the tattooed woman. He thinks "I
smiled at the tattooed woman once before and the tattooed

woman didn't smile at me." Robert walks to the vitamin section. He looks at containers of vitamins. A young woman says "So I told him, like, you're not coming home with me until you can tell me what's going on, you know?"

Another young woman says "Yeah?"

The first young woman says "Yeah it's like, I let him sleep on my bed, you know? I don't let a lot of guys do that." Robert thinks "Is one of those girls Jill?"

The second young woman says "What, do you like make them sleep on the floor?" Robert looks at a container of vitamins. He thinks "Are these the vitamins I got before? Is one of those girls Jill?"

The first young woman laughs. She says "No... I just like, don't take that many guys home." Robert looks at the container of vitamins. The first young woman says "That would be pretty funny though, making him sleep on the floor." Robert walks to the produce section. Robert turns around. He looks at the young women. The young women look at Robert. Neither of the young women is Jill. Robert picks up two bananas. He picks up a container of cashews. Robert picks up a container of mulberries. He looks at the container of mulberries. He puts down the container of mulberries. Robert walks to the cash register. The first young woman is standing behind the cash register. Robert thinks "Oh, I guess she works here." Robert thinks "What happened to the tattooed woman?"

Robert is sitting on his bed. Tom is sitting near Robert's laptop computer. Tom is looking at Robert's laptop computer. Robert says "Should I call Nancy?"

Tom says "Yeah call Nancy." Robert calls Nancy.

Robert says "I got you a fake Gucci fanny pack. Do you want to come over?"

Nancy says "No, I'm sick. Are you with Tom?"

Robert says "Yeah."

Nancy says "You guys should just come over here."

Robert says "Okay."

Nancy says "Bring soy milk and cookies and beer."

Robert says "Okay, bye." Robert says "Do you want to go to Nancy's and bring soy milk and cookies and beer?"

Tom says "Yeah okay." Robert and Tom put on shoes, coats, hats, scarves and gloves. Robert picks up a fake Gucci fanny pack. Robert and Tom walk outside. It's cold. They walk to Pathmark. Robert picks up a container of Pathmark brand organic soy milk. Robert thinks "There might be organic cookies in the natural foods aisle." Robert and Tom walk to the natural foods aisle. There are no organic cookies in the natural foods aisle. Robert and Tom look at Pathmark brand cookies. Robert and Tom talk. Robert picks up a package of Pathmark brand cookies. Tom picks up a package of Pathmark brand cookies. Robert pays for the soy milk and cookies. Robert and Tom walk outside.

Robert says "Who was that girl in *Fight Club*?" Robert and Tom are walking.

Tom says "Helena Bonham Carter."

Robert says "Oh yeah." He says "She was sexy. She looked really fucked up in that movie."

Tom says "Yeah she did." He says "Is that your type?"
Robert says "I guess."

Tom says "Yeah." He says "I was thinking about that.
I don't think I have a type. Do you have a type?"

Robert says "I don't know." Robert says "Yeah, I guess.
But, like, it doesn't really matter because I'm always drunk."
Tom says "Yeah you are."

Robert says "So there are things that I would look for
or whatever, but usually it doesn't come up." Robert and
Tom walk. Robert says "And then I'm kind of with the
person to some degree for a little while. And then the cycle
repeats itself."

Tom says "I was thinking about that." He says "How
like, sometimes if I want like, company or something, I kind
of have to drink." They walk.

Robert says "It doesn't matter, I think." Robert says
"Do you want to get beer?" They walk into a beer store.
Tom buys a six-pack of sixteen-ounce cans of Pabst Blue
Ribbon beer. Robert and Tom walk to Nancy's building.
Tom calls Nancy.

Tom says "We're outside." The door opens. Nancy
walks outside. She hugs Tom. She hugs Robert. Robert,
Tom and Nancy walk into Nancy's building. They walk up
stairs. They walk into Nancy's apartment. They walk into
Nancy's bedroom. Robert, Tom and Nancy talk. Robert
hands the fake Gucci fanny pack to Nancy. Robert, Tom
and Nancy talk.

Nancy says "Oh yeah I'm sick. So I'll get glasses for soymilk." Nancy leaves. Robert and Tom sit on Nancy's bed. Robert looks at Nancy's bedroom. Nancy walks into her bedroom. She is carrying three glasses. Nancy sits on her bed. She opens the soy milk. She pours soy milk into the glasses. Robert, Tom and Nancy eat cookies. They drink soy milk. They drink beer. Nancy puts the DVD *Gimme Shelter* into her DVD player. She turns on her TV. *Gimme Shelter* is on TV. Robert, Tom and Nancy look at the TV. On TV, The Rolling Stones are in a room. On TV, the song "Wild Horses" is playing.

Robert says "This is my favorite song ever."

Nancy says "Yeah?"

Robert says "Yeah."

Robert makes a playlist on iTunes. The first song is "Heartbeats (Live)" by The Knife. The second song is "Sway" by The Rolling Stones. The third song is "Stockholm Syndrome" by Yo La Tengo. The fourth song is "Anyway That You Want Me" by Spiritualized. The fifth song is "Step Into The Breeze (Part 1)" by Spiritualized. The sixth song is "Feel So Sad (7" Single Version)" by Spiritualized.

Robert walks. Robert is near a Chinese restaurant. He looks at the Chinese restaurant. There are people inside the Chinese restaurant. Robert thinks "I miss Alison, I guess." Robert touches his back pocket. He looks at his cell phone. Robert thinks "Should I buy an iPhone? I think I have enough money in my checking account to buy an iPhone." Robert is frowning. He is in front of his building. He walks into his building. He opens his mailbox. He looks into his mailbox. There is nothing in his mailbox. Robert closes his mailbox. He walks up stairs. He walks into his apartment. It's dark. Robert turns on the overhead light. Robert says "Hello." He puts cat food into a bowl. Robert puts water into a bowl. He checks his email. He has two new emails. Robert takes a shower. He puts on pants. He puts on shoes. He puts on a shirt. He takes off the shirt. Robert puts on a shirt. Robert checks his email. He has no new email. Robert thinks "I should shave." Robert brushes his teeth. He takes out his contact lenses. Robert plays the album *Lambent Material* by Eluvium. He turns off the overhead light. He lies on his bed. He turns off the bedside lamp. Robert opens the window.

Robert walks into his apartment. He looks at his bike. He thinks "I want to go to art school." He thinks "It would be really interesting if I were to go to art school right now. I'm not going to go to art school." He walks into his bedroom. He checks his email. He walks into the living room. He picks up his cat. He looks at his cat. Robert's cat makes a sound. Robert walks into his bedroom. He puts his cat on his bed. Robert looks at his cat. He thinks "I want my cat to like me more." Robert picks up a brush. He brushes his cat. His cat raises its back. Robert hears a car door slam shut.

Robert's phone rings. Robert answers his phone. Tom says that he's outside. Robert says something. He walks out of his apartment. He opens his building door. Tom walks into Robert's building. Robert and Tom hug.

Tom says "Hi."

Robert says "Hey man, what's up." Robert and Tom walk up stairs. They walk into Robert's apartment.

Tom says "Just chillin', you know."

Robert says "Yeah I don't know." He says "What'd you do tonight?"

Tom says "I was at Olivia's. She gave me a ride over."

Robert says "She has a car?"

Tom says "She has her mom's car for some reason."

Robert says "Nice."

Tom says "Yeah." Robert and Tom walk into Robert's bedroom. Tom says "Is it okay if I sleep here tonight?"

Robert says "Yeah man. Always."

Tom says "Thanks man." Robert checks his email. Tom picks up a blanket. He puts the blanket on the floor. He puts a pillow on the floor. Tom lies on the blanket on the floor. Robert and Tom talk.

Robert says "Do you have work tomorrow?"

Tom says "Yeah, at nine."

Robert says "To five?"

Tom says "Something like that." Tom says "Do you?"

Robert says "Yeah."

Tom says "Yeah."

Robert says "Yeah." Robert reads an email. He writes two emails. Robert looks at Tom. Tom's eyes are closed. Robert says "*Ay bay bay*." Robert walks to the bathroom. He pees. He washes his face. Robert brushes his teeth. He walks to his bedroom. He turns off the overhead light.

Robert is lying on his bed. The window is open. It's cold. Robert is wearing a sweater. The sweater is black. The sweater is wool. Robert looks out the window. He sees houses and wires. Robert looks at his bedroom. He sees a chair, a t-shirt and an issue of *Vice* magazine. Robert looks at the overhead light. He thinks "I drank a lot last night. More than I should have."

Robert says "Xiu Xiu is cool."
    Tom says "Yeah?"
    Robert says "Yeah, they're funny. I like Xiu Xiu. I like their lyrics."
    Tom says "Do you think that guy feels, like, weird all the time?"
    Robert says "I don't know. He probably feels really happy. He's probably really rich."
    Tom says "What's his name?"
    Robert says "Jamie Somers or something. Jamie Stewart."
    Tom says "He's probably not that rich."
    Robert says "Yeah he is."
    Tom says "How?"

Robert says "They're like one of the most popular indie bands right now, and they have a lot of records. I don't know. He's probably as rich as Devendra Banhart. He's richer than Diplo. They're in magazines all the time and tour and stuff. I don't know. They're good at merchandising. They have, like, limited edition photo books and stuff. They're really good at making money."

Tom says "Yeah." He says "Do you think he feels weird when he sings, though?"

Robert says "What?"

Tom says "Do you think that guy feels weird when he's singing?"

Robert says "He probably feels awesome. He's probably on, like, really strong muscle relaxers. He's so rich. He probably pays someone to blog for him."

Tom says "He doesn't sound happy. On his records, I mean."

Robert says "That's just so people will think he's cool and buy stuff." Robert says "He's so rich. He's probably so happy." Robert looks at a newspaper.

Tom says "Does he sound happy on the new one?"

Robert says "He sounds shitty. He sounds like shit."

Tom says "That sucks."

Robert says "Maybe they won't sell any records and then he won't have money and he'll feel really sad and make another good record."

Tom says "Yeah, that would be cool."

Robert calls Alison. He's standing up. Robert thinks "Alison." Robert doesn't leave a voicemail. He sits on his bed. His back is against the wall. The album *Sharpen Your Teeth* by Ugly Casanova is playing.

Nancy is holding a brown paper bag. Robert and Nancy walk up five flights of stairs. Robert knocks on a door. Robert says "I hear things moving inside. I hear someone shuffling cards maybe." The door opens. Nancy hugs Salma.

Nancy says "Robert, this is Salma. Salma, Robert."

Robert says "How do you do?" Robert puts out his hand. Robert and Salma shake hands. Robert and Nancy walk into Salma's apartment. There is a small dog. Robert sits on a chair. Nancy sits on the floor. Robert sees Sam. Robert says "Hi Sam."

Sam says "Hi Robert." Sam is eating edamame.

Robert sees a young woman. Robert says "Who are you?"

The young woman says "Margot." Salma walks into the room. She has a corkscrew. Nancy takes a bottle of wine out of the brown paper bag. Nancy hands the bottle of wine to Salma. Salma opens the bottle of wine. The movie *The Ice Storm* is playing.

Robert says "We should watch *Garden State*." Sam smiles. Robert says "It's my birthday." Salma says that she doesn't want to watch *Garden State*. Robert asks Margot what her favorite band is. Margot says she doesn't have a favorite band. Margot looks at Salma. Margot asks Robert what his favorite band is. Robert says "Pavement." The movie *Garden State* is playing.

Salma says "So what do you do?"

Robert says "I'm an actor. I mean, that's my passion."

Salma says "Really?"

Nancy says "No it isn't." Robert looks at Nancy. Everyone drinks wine. Robert says that he has to leave. Robert walks outside.

Robert calls Alison. He doesn't leave a voicemail. He sends her a text message. The text message says "hi."

The album *Something About Airplanes* by Death Cab for Cutie is playing. Robert thinks "I'm getting less and less cool as I get older. I'm not even old at all but I'm not cool anymore. Does being cool matter less to me now? What's happening? If I stopped focusing on being cool why haven't I started focusing on something else?"

Robert plays the song "William, It Was Really Nothing" by The Smiths. Robert's cell phone rings. Robert pauses the music. He looks at his cell phone. He presses the green button on his cell phone. He puts his cell phone to his ear. Robert says "Hello." Alison says "Hello." Robert hears voices in the background. Alison says "Sorry I was speaking so quietly this morning. Mike was asleep and I didn't want to wake him up."

Robert says "That's okay." He says "That's kind of what I thought."

Alison says "What?"

Robert says "That's okay," a little louder.

Alison says "Do you feel depressed?"

Robert says "Yes."

Alison says "About Mike?"

Robert says "I don't know." He says "About you. Sort of."

Alison says "Oh." Robert moves his cell phone from his right ear to his left ear. Alison says "I'm sorry I've been such a bad friend to you."

Robert says "It's okay." He is crying quietly. He says "You haven't." He says "What are you talking about?"

Alison says "I'm sorry I don't know how to make you feel better."

Robert says "No, that's okay."

Alison says "What?" Robert takes his cell phone away from his ear. He presses the red button on his cell phone. Robert connects his cell phone to his cell phone charger. He plays the song "William, It Was Really Nothing" by The Smiths.

Robert looks at his laptop computer. Nancy is on Gmail. Nancy says "Hi."

Robert says "Hi."

Nancy says "How are you?"

Robert says "Good. I watched TV today." Robert says "How are you?"

Nancy says "Good." Nancy says "Are you my friend?"

Robert says "Yeah." He spells it "yeaj."

Nancy says "Good." She says "That makes me happy." She says "I've been having this paranoia lately that all my friends hate me and it makes me feel anxious."

Robert says "Nope."

Robert walks out of a subway station. Robert is walking. Robert calls Alison. He says "Hi."

Alison says "Hi, are you here?"

Robert says "Yeah I'm—oh nevermind, I see you." Robert puts his cell phone into his pocket. He walks to Alison's building. Alison is standing on her stoop. Two other people are standing on Alison's stoop. Alison is smoking a cigarette. Alison drops her cigarette. Alison walks into her building. Robert walks into Alison's building. Robert looks at Alison. Robert says "Hi."

Alison says "Hi." Alison unlocks her apartment door. Robert and Alison walk into Alison's apartment. Robert and Alison walk into Alison's bedroom. Robert turns on the overhead light. Robert looks at Alison. Alison laughs quietly. Robert opens his book bag.

Robert says "I got you something. A long time ago."

Alison says "Oh. Thank you." Robert takes an envelope out of his book bag. Robert hands the envelope to Alison.

Alison says "Thank you." She takes a piece of paper out of the envelope. The piece of paper has four pictures on it. The pictures are of a woman holding a baby. The pictures have captions. Alison says "This is a different one than I saw that time. The other one only had 'The correct way to hold a baby' and 'The incorrect way to hold a baby.' This is good. I like this. Thank you. I'll frame it and put it on my wall."

Robert says "I was going to frame it for you, but then we stopped being friends." Alison laughs quietly. Robert says "I'm glad you like it."

Alison says "I have these for you." Alison hands Robert the books *The Other Side of the Mountain* by Michel Bernanos and *The Luck of Roaring Camp and Other Stories* by Bret Harte.

Robert says "Thank you." He puts the books into his book bag. He closes his book bag. Robert looks at Alison. Robert says "What happened?" Alison puts the piece of paper in the envelope.

Alison says "I don't know. The last couple times we talked on the phone. I don't think I ever knew what was happening." Robert stands up. Alison says "I have a paper due in two hours."

Robert says "Do you need to work on your paper?"

Alison says "I'm going to start at four. It's due two hours from four." Robert looks at Alison's cell phone.

Robert says "We have thirty-eight minutes."

Alison says "Yeah." Robert looks at Alison's laptop computer. Alison's laptop computer's wallpaper is a picture of Alison and someone kissing.

Robert says "Is Mike your boyfriend?"

Alison says "I don't know. I don't even know. He

doesn't talk to me sometimes. Like he hasn't talked to me since we hung out last."

Robert says "Did you have sex with Mike?"

Alison says "Yeah." Alison looks at the ceiling. Robert looks at the ceiling. Robert looks at a poster for a Modest Mouse concert in Seattle. He looks at Alison.

Robert says "You like Modest Mouse?" Alison laughs. Robert laughs. They talk.

Alison says "Your jeans are really tight." She laughs.

Robert says "Yeah." He says "Yeah. I should go." Robert walks to Alison's apartment door. Alison walks to her apartment door. Robert opens Alison's apartment door. Robert walks to Alison's building door. Robert looks at Alison. Robert and Alison walk onto Alison's stoop. Robert looks at Alison. Alison lights a cigarette. Robert says "I wish we wanted the same thing."

Alison says "Whenever we wanted the same thing, you didn't want it."

Robert says "Yeah." He says "I don't know." Robert looks at Alison.

Alison says "I really tried to be your girlfriend. I really wanted to be your girlfriend for a long time." Alison says "But I don't know." Robert looks at Alison. She looks at Robert.

Robert says "I'm sorry." He looks at Alison. He looks at his shoes. Robert says "I guess we can't... start over?"

Alison says "I don't... I don't think so. I have Mike, or something. And I think everything is just fucked."

Robert says "Yeah." He looks at his cell phone. He says "It's 4:02. You have to write your paper." He looks at Alison.

Alison says "Yeah. Are you going home?"

Robert says "Yeah." Robert walks.

Alison says "Bye." Robert stops walking. He looks at Alison.

Robert says "If you ever want..." quietly.

Alison says "What?" Robert looks at Alison.

Robert says "Huh?"

Alison says "You said something. What did you say?"

Robert says "Nothing."

Alison says "You said something. What did you say?"

Robert says "Nothing." Alison looks at Robert.

Robert says "I just said that if you ever want to hang out sometime. I don't know." Robert walks.

Alison says "Okay. Bye." Robert is crying.

Robert is eating nori. The album *The Reminder* by Feist is playing. He looks at his bedroom floor. There are four empty Red Stripe Lager bottles on Robert's bedroom floor. There are eight neckties on Robert's bedroom floor. There is a black Members Only jacket on Robert's bedroom floor. Robert emails Alison. He says "I'm bored."

Alison emails Robert. Alison says "I'm in bed singing along to Death Cab for Cutie." Robert plays the album *The Photo Album* by Death Cab For Cutie.

Robert says "I listened to Feist. I don't like Feist I think. I'm listening to Death Cab for Cutie now. *The Photo Al-*

bum." Robert thinks "Alison is listening to *Transatlanticism*." He thinks "*Transatlanticism* sucks." Robert says "I'm eating nori."

Alison says "Oh. Good. What are you doing"

Robert says "I don't know. I searched Craigslist personals for 'New Order' and nothing came up. Then I searched 'Minor Threat' and nothing came up. There are a lot of results for 'indie.' I feel depressed. I'm going to read all of the results for 'indie' that I haven't read already."

Alison says "I was on Craigslist for like an hour last night. It was depressing."

Robert says "I searched '*The Squid and the Whale*,' then 'Ann Beattie,' then 'Yates,' then 'Yves Saint Laurent.'" He says "There were no results."

Alison says "Do you want to sleep over?" She says "I'm leaving Thursday."

Sam says "What would make you feel happy right now?" Robert and Sam are walking. It's night.

Robert says "Nothing." He says "No, I don't know. Drinking beer while lying down. Either one of those." Robert and Sam walk past a strip club. Robert says "I just want to be crying in someone's arms." There is a red light. Robert and Sam stop walking.

Sam says "I want that, too." The light becomes green. Sam says "It just has to be the right arms."

ZACHARY GERMAN was born on December 17th, 1988 at Shore Memorial Hospital in Somer's Point, New Jersey. In 2006 he dropped out of high school. In 2007 he published his first short story. In 2008 he moved to Brooklyn. In 2009 he works as a dog walker on Manhattan's Upper West Side and maintains two websites: thingswhatibought. com, and eatwhenyoufeelsad.com, which collects videos of people eating while feeling sad.